We finished in perfect harmony, the last chord hanging there in the air.

We sounded great. And Jane had written a hell of a tune. I opened my eyes to tell her, but before I could say a word, someone else spoke up.

"That was a thing of beauty," said the deep baritone voice. I looked up, and my heart stopped. Because standing there in the doorway was a face I had only seen in the picture that was now under my pillow, the face with my almond-shaped eyes, smiling my smile.

It was Monroe LaCrue.

It was my father.

Books by Cherie Bennett

Wild Hearts
Wild Hearts on Fire
Wild Hearts Forever
Wild Hearts on the Edge

Available from ARCHWAY Paperbacks

WILD HEARTS on the Edge

CHERIE BENNETT

AN ARCHWAY PAPERBACK
Published by POCKET BOOKS
New York   London   Toronto   Sydney   Tokyo   Singapore

AN ARCHWAY PAPERBACK *Original*

 An Archway Paperback published by
POCKET BOOKS, a division of Simon & Schuster Inc.
1230 Avenue of the Americas, New York, NY 10020

Copyright © 1994 by Cherie Bennett

ISBN: 0-671-88781-5

First Archway Paperback printing August 1994

10 9 8 7 6 5 4 3 2 1

AN ARCHWAY PAPERBACK and colophon are registered trademarks of Simon & Schuster Inc.

Cover photo by Media Photo Group

Printed in the U.S.A.

IL: 7+

*For Matt Carlton and Sandra Smith
Carlton—true friends forever*

CHAPTER
1

The movie was great, huh, Sandra?" my boyfriend Darryl Waverly, said as we walked into Musical Burgers, our favorite place in all of Nashville for a good, cheap meal. It's right near the campus of Vanderbilt University and it's always crowded with students, musicians, songwriters, and wanna-be's.

"Oh, yeah," I replied distractedly as Darryl took my hand and we made our way through the crowd to the only unoccupied table in sight.

"Especially the part where the actress took off all her clothes and ran naked into the subway," Darryl elaborated.

"What?"

"And the part where the little kid chopped his teacher up into a zillion pieces and fried him over an open campfire," Darryl went on with relish. "Yum-yum!"

"What are you talking about?" I asked him. "It was a British movie about class oppression—there wasn't even a little kid or a naked woman or a subway in it . . . I don't think."

"But you're not sure," Darryl pointed out.

"I'm sure," I insisted, even though I really wasn't sure at all.

"Well, good," Darryl said. "For a while there I thought you were planet-hopping through the entire flick."

"Very funny," I replied, opening the menu. Then I closed it again. "I don't know why I'm looking at this thing, I know it by heart."

Darryl reached over and took my hands in his. "What's up, babe? You've been somewhere else all night."

"Yeah, I guess," I admitted with a sigh. "I'm just strung out, I guess. Too much to do, too little time to do it."

Darryl grinned at me. He has this incredible grin. "You just need to make a schedule and follow it."

"I know that, Mr. Organized," I said irritably, pulling my hands away from his. "I *have* a schedule and I *do* follow it."

He reached for me again. "If you think I'm going to let your bad mood spoil tonight, you're wrong. I don't get to see you often enough to waste a night on bickering."

He was right. How could I?

A friend of Darryl's from Fisk University—Darryl is a freshman there, straight A's, pre-med—came up to talk to him, and I watched Darryl's face, and wondered how I'd see him if I didn't know him. It was tough. Darryl has been my boyfriend since I was in seventh grade and he was in ninth grade. I tried to study him objectively, and even objectively he was totally fine—golden brown skin the color of graham crackers, huge brown eyes with the longest eyelashes, and a smile to die for. Slim. With muscles. And gorgeous hands with long, masculine, finely tapered fingers—perfect for a future doctor who would help make people well.

But what was more important was, I knew the Darryl he was on the inside—really good and honest and fine. He wanted to be a doctor to help poor kids, especially poor black kids, and so did I.

But sometimes I wondered . . . what would it be like to date someone else? I had never gone out with anyone but Darryl, never even really kissed anyone but Darryl. We had our future all mapped out—I would finish high school, we'd both go to medical school, and then we'd open a practice together in Nashville, get married, and live happily ever after.

It was a good plan, right? And I really loved Darryl. But . . . but what, I don't know. He's so . . . so perfect—perfectly organized, perfectly smart, perfectly analytical.

And sometimes I didn't like having my whole life planned out at the ripe old age of sixteen.

I didn't tell Darryl that part. How could I? You see, he would just blame it on the fact that I'd become the bass player for this all-girl country rock band, Wild Hearts. Darryl thought the band was a waste of my time, and he wasn't too thrilled that all the other girls in the band were white, either. He also thought they were a bad influence on me. He actually used that phrase—"a bad influence." It made my skin feel prickly, because it sounds like he's someone's forty-five-year-old father smoking a damn pipe or something. Like you'd expect the next words out of his mouth to be "when I was your age. . . ."

But the fact of the matter is, I liked being

in the band. Everyone thought of me as being so pragmatic and goal-oriented—I liked doing something kind of wild for a change. So there I was, president of the junior class at Green Hills High, captain of the tennis team, top student in our class academically with my future all planned out, except . . . except that I was in this wild band. And I loved it.

"Did I tell you how pretty you look tonight?" Darryl asked me.

"Huh?" was my stellar response, since I'd been completely lost in thought. "I thought you were still talking to Raymond."

"He walked away about two minutes ago," Darryl said. He reached for my hand again. "He said bye to you and you didn't even hear him."

"Sorry," I mumbled.

"He said you looked pretty, too," Darryl added.

I had to smile. He was trying so hard. Sometimes I got mad at him because he never complimented me. I could see my reflection in the mirror by our booth—short, natural hair, deep-set almond-shaped brown eyes, chocolate-colored skin, my mother's good cheekbones, and a nice long neck. I had on a white cotton shirt with an embroidered vest, jeans, and hiking boots. I knew I looked fit, since I taught aerobics part-time after school and I loved to jog and play tennis. All in all, I was reasonably satisfied with the way I looked. Not devastating, maybe, but nice.

It would be fun to be devastating, though, just once.

That side of me—the I'd-like-to-be-devastating side—well, I don't show that to many people. Correction. *Any* people.

A new waitress came over to the table and we ordered Chinese chicken salads, then I idly looked through the tunes on the jukebox selector at the table.

"Oh, there's 'It Wasn't God Who Made Honky Tonk Angels'!" I noted. "Did I tell you Wild Hearts is covering that?"

Darryl frowned. "What is it?"

I grinned. Darryl knows less about country music than anyone else in Nashville. "It's an old country standard by Kitty Wells. Savy worked up this great arrangement for us. We do it very rocked-out in four-part harmony."

"That's nice," Darryl said, making it pretty clear he couldn't care less. "Hey, how did you do on that advanced calculus test? You never did tell me," he said, changing the subject.

"We've got new outfits for this big Battle

of the Bands that's coming up," I continued, ignoring his question about calculus. His attitude toward the band really ticked me off.

He made a face. "Sandra, what is more important to you, calculus or that lame band?"

"The band," I snapped. I didn't know if it was true or not, but I was in an ornery mood.

"Sandra . . ." Darryl said in a warning voice.

"I got a C on that stupid calculus test, for your information," I blurted out, "so I guess the band must be more important!"

I hadn't intended to tell him. But it was really, really preying on my mind. In fact, that's what I was so upset about. My first C. Ever.

Darryl just stared at me in shock. "I would have helped you study," he finally said in a gentle voice.

I ran my hand over my hair and sighed. "I know that, honey," I said softly. "I just . . . I messed up. I can't believe I did that."

"Well, so, you're not perfect," Darryl said, struggling to find the right thing to say. "Will it bring down your A for the semester?"

"No, Ms. Packwood has this system where she throws out the lowest test score, so I'm okay."

The waitress brought us our salads, but suddenly I wasn't hungry. How could I have messed up that test? I just hadn't had time to study. I had been too busy. I knew I was a perfectionist (it drove my mother crazy—she is a laid-back ex-hippie—we are definitely opposites) but being a perfectionist had always worked for me in the past.

Yeah. The past. But it wasn't working for me now.

"Sandra honey, is that you?" my stepdad called to me from the living room when I came in the front door after my date.

"Yeah," I replied. I was surprised he was up. My stepfather, Lawrence-don't-call-me-Larry, is a truly great guy, but he is seriously by-the-books. He's an accountant and—gasp—a Republican. Every single night he has a glass of warm milk at ten o'clock, and then he goes to bed. My mom, Lori, on the other hand, stays up until all hours. She's a singer, and she sings backup and does demos for the biggest stars in Nashville. She's also a liberal Democrat. Yet the two of them are crazy about each other—definite proof that opposites attract.

I wandered into the living room and got my second surprise—my mom was sitting there with Larry (I call him Larry, because I always knew I had a birth father somewhere or other, and because I'm the only one in the whole world that he allows to call him by a nickname), and they were both drinking wine. My parents don't drink. And the two of them had that We Are Very Concerned look on their faces that strikes fear in the hearts of teens everywhere.

Oh, God. Somehow they had found out about that C on the calculus test. That had to be it. It wouldn't bother my mother very much—she thinks I'm much too perfectionistic and driven as it is. But Larry, he would be really disappointed in me.

"What's up?" I asked cautiously, sitting in the chair opposite them.

"How was your date?" my mother asked.

"Fine," I replied.

"And how is Darryl?" Larry asked.

I cocked my head to the side. "Somehow I don't think the two of you stayed up drinking wine so you could ask me about Darryl, right?"

They looked at each other.

"It's about the test, right?" I blurted out. I looked at Larry. "I know. I completely messed up. It'll never happen again. What did Darryl do, call you from the restaurant and tell you?" Then an even worse thought crossed my mind.

"Oh, no, Ms. Packwood didn't actually call you, did she?"

They looked confused.

"What are you talking about?" my mother finally said. "What test?"

"This isn't about my calculus test?"

"No," Larry replied. I waited for him to follow up with the obvious—what calculus test and how badly had I done on it—but he never said a word.

That's when I got really scared.

"What is it?" I asked them. "Is someone sick? You're making me very nervous."

My mother took a long sip of her wine. "Well, baby, we had an . . . interesting phone call while you were out."

"Actually, the call was for you," Larry said in his perfectly modulated tones.

"From who?"

They looked at each other again.

"Your father," my mom finally said.

I couldn't have been more surprised if she'd said "The pope." I had a photo of my father, and that was about it. He and my mother had divorced when I was four, and he'd left for Europe when I was six. He was a jazz pianist, that much I knew, and he'd gone to Europe to pursue a career that was getting nowhere in the United States. My mother didn't talk about him very much, but I knew what she thought of him. He was a loser, seriously bad news. She'd been seduced by his good looks and his talent. From the little I knew about him, I wanted to make sure I was nothing at all like him. In all these years he'd never sent me a card or a letter, and he'd certainly never called me. I had decided a long time before that he'd obviously written me off, and so I'd written him off, too.

"Gee, how sweet of him," I said sarcastically when I could find my voice. "How did he even find me?" We'd moved to Nashville from Detroit a few years earlier because my mom could get more vocal work in Nashville.

"He called your grandmother in Detroit, I gather," my mom said.

"Well, Mother Pearl shouldn't have given him our number," I said, getting up. "I'm going to bed."

"He wants to see you," my mother said. That stopped me in my tracks halfway to the door.

I turned around. "Well, I don't want to see him."

"He said it was important," Larry said.

I folded my arms and stared at Larry. "Do you think I should see him?"

Larry thought a moment. "I think this is a decision you must make for yourself," he finally said.

"Good, I've made it," I said.

"Maybe you should think about it," my mother suggested mildly.

"Why is he calling now?" I asked, stress coloring my voice. "I didn't ask him to come into my life after all these years." No one said anything. "Look, my life is perfectly planned out, and he is definitely not a part of it." I looked at Larry. "Besides, I have a father!"

Larry smiled gratefully. "I know that, baby. But maybe there's some . . . some compelling reason for his calling you after all these years."

"Well, maybe I don't care about his 'compelling reason,' " I shot back.

My mother pushed a sheet of paper toward me. It read "Monroe LaCrue" with a local phone number and a room number.

I picked it up. "He's *here?*" I cried. "In *Nashville?*"

"He's staying downtown at the Doubletree Hotel," my mother said.

"He has no damn right to be in Nashville," I exploded.

"He said he'd be there for one week," my mother continued. "He said to call him if you'll see him—he's leaving it up to you. He said to tell you he'd be there a week, waiting to hear from you."

I stuffed the paper into my pocket. "Well, he's gonna have a long damn wait, as far as I'm concerned," I muttered. I walked over and kissed my parents good night, then I ran up to my room.

My father. After all these years.

I looked at the photo next to my bed, taken so many years ago. He was young then. I had his almond-shaped eyes and his smile. I traced that smile with my finger, wondering why he wanted to come into my life now.

Knock-knock-knock.

"Come in," I called, quickly turning the photograph face-down.

It was Larry. He came over and sat next to me on my bed. "I want you to know, sweetie, it's okay with me if you want to see your father. I won't be hurt."

I took his hand. "He's not my father. You are," I said.

Tears came to Larry's eyes, and he quickly turned away from me, hoping I wouldn't see. "You know I couldn't love you any more than I do," he said in a muffled voice.

"Don't worry," I told Larry earnestly. "This

guy can wait by the phone from now until hell freezes over, and he isn't going to hear from me."

Larry stood up, then he leaned over and kissed my forehead. "You are some terrific young woman," he told me in a voice gruff with emotion. I could see him fighting to get control of himself. He cleared his throat. "Now, what is this about a calculus test?"

I sighed. "I got a C on a calculus test. My first C."

"You didn't prepare, I take it," Larry said.

"You take it right," I admitted.

"Well, it seems to me you know exactly what to do to alter that situation in the future," Larry explained.

"Yeah," I agreed. "I've just been so busy— too busy! I used to be able to keep on top of everything . . ."

"But that's getting more difficult," Larry finished for me.

I nodded in agreement.

"Prioritize," Larry suggested.

"I know, I will," I promised. I shook my head in disgust. "I can't believe I actually got a C."

Larry smiled. "I got a C once, too. I felt humiliated and told no one. And I never forgot it."

I laughed. "I bet you didn't. Well, don't worry, your secret is safe with me." I reached out for Larry's hand. "We're just alike, you and I, aren't we?"

He squeezed my fingers. "We are, at that," he replied with pride. "And no father could be prouder of his daughter. Good night."

Larry left, and I picked up the photo of my father and dumped it into the wastepaper basket. Who needed him?

But in the middle of the night, somewhere in that twilight zone between being completely asleep and completely awake, I got up and retrieved that photo, and I put it under my pillow.

I had no idea why.

CHAPTER 2

Is that all you're eating for lunch?" Savy Leeman asked me the next day as she walked over to our usual table in the cafeteria.

Savy is the lead singer and keyboard player of Wild Hearts. I suppose in a way it's her band—she's the one who brought all of us together. I really like Savy, I always have, although we weren't close friends until the band. She's a little plump thing with lots of curly red hair and enough enthusiasm for any ten people. And she is a truly talented musician.

"Don't worry, Mom," I teased her. "I'm fine." I spooned the last of a low-fat yogurt into my mouth.

She made a face at me and opened her own brown bag, which I knew would have something great in it. Her grandmother—we all call her Gramma Beth—is this incredibly cool woman in her seventies (and the best fiddle player I know), and she fed the entire Leeman family as if every meal would be their last. When Savy pulled out a soggy liverwurst sandwich, I remembered that Gramma Beth was in the hospital, that she might have to have brain surgery. I had been so wrapped up in my own life that I'd forgotten. In fact, we were all supposed to go visit her in the hospital that day after school. I sighed. I really wanted to visit Gramma Beth, but I really needed to study, especially since we were having band practice that night.

"How's Gramma Beth?" I asked Savy as she bit gingerly into her unappetizing sandwich.

"Good news," Savy reported, making a face at the food in her mouth and gulping it down. "She's getting out of the hospital today."

"That's fabulous!" I exclaimed. "But what about—"

"The tumor?" Savy said. "It's there, but not too big. And it's not threatening anything at the moment. So the doctors said they're going to watch it and see if it grows."

I shuddered. "That's a gruesome thought."

"What is, this school?" Jane asked, plopping down into the seat next to me. She made a face at Savy. "What are you eating, dog food on rye?"

Jane is Wild Hearts' drummer. She just moved to Nashville from New York City. Against her will, I might add. Her dad got transferred here, and she was major bummed out about it. I like her. She's very funny and original, and a really great drummer. But she has this thing about her looks. She dresses in costumes half the time—one day she's a geisha girl, another day she's punked out with green in her hair, whatever. It's not a very good way to win friends and influence people, if you ask me. Some of the kids at school rank on her about it. Of course, those kids are idiots, but why give people ammunition to use against you?

"It's not dog food, as you so eloquently put it," Savy said. "It's some kind of liver pâté stuff."

Jane stuck her tongue out. "Gag me with a spoon." She looked around. "Where's Kimmy? She said she'd look over the rough draft of my research paper on Freud." She shook her head with disgust. "Freud. Can you believe it? Like the guy wasn't totally sexist."

Savy cocked her head across the room. "Kimmy's sitting with Sawyer over there," she reported.

I looked across the room, and there was Kimmy Carrier, our lead guitar player, laughing with her new—and very first—boyfriend, Sawyer Paxton. Recently we'd done a makeover on Kimmy—she was always hiding her light under a bushel basket, as my grandmother used to say. She was finally beginning to come out of her shell. That was a relief, because Kimmy was the shyest, most insecure girl I had ever met. You know, the type who apologizes for breathing. And she never had anything to apologize *for!* She was blessed with great looks—tall, blond, thin, and curvy—a first-class brain, and incredible talent on the guitar. Oh, and another thing, she's rich. I mean, heiress-type rich. You'd think with all of that the girl would get some ego strength instead of doing this "poor me" routine.

"Ah, young lust," Jane sighed. "Not that I remember lust. I mean, it's been so long since I had a meaningful encounter with an actual guy." She popped up. "I'm getting some food. Will you look at my Freud paper, Sandra?"

"Can't," I replied. "I have to get over to the student council office." I threw my yogurt container at the garbage can. "Basket!" I cried, when it circled the rim and fell in.

"Practice is tonight at seven, okay?" Savy called to me as I headed for the door.

"I'm there," I assured her. I walked briskly down to the student council office and looked at my in-box. There was a note from the junior class secretary, Jennie Neuman: "We need to meet tonight about homecoming. How's my house, eight o'clock? Jennie."

"No way," I muttered, scribbling a note back to her. She walked in just as I was writing.

"Oh, you got my note?" she asked me.

"Yeah. I can't meet tonight," I told her.

"But we've got this problem about juniors on the football team whose grade-point falls below a two-oh," Jennie explained. "They want to play in the homecoming game, which is clearly against school rules. We have to figure out where we stand."

"Well, we'll just have to figure it out some other time," I said. "I'm busy."

Jennie put her books on her desk and folded her arms. "Sandra, you are the president of the junior class," she reminded me—like I needed reminding. "This is your responsibility."

She sounded entirely too much like Darryl.

"I know that, Jennie," I said, trying not to sound as irritated as I felt. "And I'll deal with it, okay?"

"When?" she asked me.

"When I get to it," I replied.

She sighed ostentatiously. "Well, all I can say is that you used to have time to do what the class elected you to do."

"I still have time," I maintained, looking through the rest of the papers in my in-box."

"I don't know," Jennie said primly. "You weren't in that band then."

I stood up and shoved the papers back into my box. "The band doesn't have anything to do with this."

Jennie gave me a supercilious look. "That's not what everyone is saying."

"What's that supposed to mean?"

"Oh, nothing," Jennie said, in a tone of voice that made it clear she thought it was a real *big* something.

"Jennie, don't play those games with me," I said testily. "If you have something to say, then just say it."

"Oh, it's not me," she assured me. "But *some* people are saying that you're spending more time on that band than on being president of the class. *Some* people are wondering if you shouldn't be replaced."

I gave her a steely look. "Well, you tell *some* people that if they have anything to say to me, they had better say it to my face," I seethed. "You got that?"

She nodded and tried to look sincere.

I knew better. Jennie Neuman wanted my job.

"Gramma Beth is home!" Savy cried when she opened her front door to my knock a few hours later.

"That's great," I said, stepping into the front hall. I noticed that part of the wallpaper had been changed again, from a blue and white pinstripe to something floral and peachy. The Leemans were constantly renovating and re-decorating their house, but somehow one room never got finished before another room got started.

"How's she feeling?"

"She keeps saying she's fine and everyone should stop making a fuss," Savy reported as we headed for the music room. She turned to look at me. "She's not fine, though."

"Well, I know that—she has a brain tumor."

"I mean she gets these bad headaches," Savy said with concern. "And sometimes she gets dizzy. Daddy doesn't want her driving. You can imagine how crazy that idea is making her."

"I don't blame her," I commiserated. I threw my jacket on the old couch, nodded to Jane and Kimmy who had already arrived, then opened my case and took out my bass guitar.

"She insists she's coming to hear us play in the Battle of the Bands Saturday night," Kimmy reported from the other side of the room, where she was tuning her guitar. "I don't think she's well enough."

"You can't keep her down," Jane decreed, running her brushes across her drums. "Can we go see her later?"

Savy shook her head no. "She took some kind of pill to make her sleep. But she says today is absolutely the last day she's taking it. She says it keeps her from thinking."

"Your grandmother is the coolest," Jane said. "I wish she was related to me."

I smiled, because I felt the same way. I only have one living grandparent, my mother's mother, who lives in Detroit. She's a schoolteacher and a deacon at the Baptist church, and she thinks I'm going to hell because I play rock and country music. We are talking strict. You can imagine what it was like for a woman like that to raise up a daughter who turned out to be a hippie and a musician. I thought again about how Mother Pearl—that's what we call her—had given our phone number to my father. The only time Mother Pearl had ever referred to my father, it was as "that heathen." So what had possessed her to even have a conversation with him?

"How about if we start with that new one Jane wrote?" Savy said, rummaging through the charts on the top of her old upright piano.

"I don't think we should do that one for the Battle of the Bands," I said.

"Why not?" Jane asked. "It's a great tune."

"It's good," I agreed. "But I think we need to be practical about this. We should do cover tunes that the judges will know."

"That's stupid!" Jane cried. "We'll never win with cover tunes!"

"Oh, we're not going to win anyway," Kimmy put in in her soft drawl.

"Ya'll cut it out!" Savy cried. "We might win, you never know! We have to have a positive attitude!"

"Look, our band has been together a few weeks," I pointed out. "We're competing against the best high school and college bands in the city, bands that have been together for years!"

"Well, so what?" Savy countered. "We're really good, and we're unique. We get to do four tunes, so how about we do two originals and two covers?"

I nodded reluctantly, as did Jane. Kimmy agreed, too.

"Okay, so that's settled," Savy said. "Let's start with 'Love's Gone Away.' "

Savy counted us off, and then we began the opening chords to Jane's latest ballad. It really was pretty, and Savy sang it great.

A long time ago
And far, far away
You loved me so well
That I thought you would stay.
I called it forever—
You called it for now.
Now love's gone away
And heartbreak takes a bow....

I closed my eyes and leaned into my vocal mike, adding a lower harmony line when we reached the chorus. Our voices were blending together so well now, the four parts tumbling and sliding over each other as we sang the poignant chorus.

Love's gone, love's gone, gone away.
Love's gone, love's gone, gone away.

I knew Jane had written this song about her old boyfriend in New York, Chad Berman, who was now hot and heavy with some other girl. But when I closed my eyes and sang those lyrics, I thought about my father, Monroe LaCrue. Surely he must have loved me when I was a little girl. I stretched my memory back until my mind hurt from searching, but I couldn't recall him holding me or singing to me or throwing me up in the air to hear my baby giggles. But maybe he had. I wished I still had those memories. Something. Something more than the name of some man who thought so little of me that he had forgotten I existed for ten damn years.

Love's gone, love's gone, gone away.
Love's gone, love's gone, gone away.

We finished in perfect harmony, the last chord hanging there in the air. We sounded great. And Jane had written a hell of a tune. I opened my eyes to tell her, but before I could say a word, someone else spoke up.

"That was a thing of beauty," said the deep baritone voice.

I looked up, and my heart stopped. Because standing there in the doorway was a man whose face I had only seen in the picture that was now under my pillow, the face with my almond-shaped eyes, smiling my smile.

It was Monroe LaCrue.

My father.

CHAPTER
3

🝙

I couldn't move, couldn't speak. It was like one of those awful nightmares where your feet are rooted to the spot and your voice is just gone. Savy, Jane, and Kimmy looked at the man standing in the doorway, who was staring right at me. Then they all looked at me expectantly, but that wasn't getting them anywhere, so they looked back at him again.

"Sorry to interrupt," Monroe finally said. "I'm Sandra's—"

"Friend," I finished for him in a forceful voice that sounded too loud to my own ears. "A friend of the family, I mean," I explained, trying to sound nonchalant. I gave Monroe—I couldn't possibly think of him as my *father*—a hard look. "What are you doing here?"

"I came to see you," he said, a look of hope and longing on his face.

My friends looked back and forth at the two of us, wondering what the hell was going on. "Excuse me just a minute," I finally said. I unhooked the strap on my bass and crossed the room into the stairwell. Monroe turned and followed me.

"What do you want?" I asked him belligerently, folding my arms.

"To see you," he said gently. His eyes searched my face, and he smiled. "You turned out beautiful, just like your momma."

"Leave her out of this," I snapped. "And just how the hell did you happen to find me at band practice?"

"I followed your Jeep from your house," he admitted. "I've been circling around this block forever, trying to get up the nerve to come inside." He gave me that grin again. "A cute little red-haired girl let me in. I told her I was your daddy."

The cute little red-haired girl would be Savy's little sister, Shelaylah, I figured. Little kids have no sense. They'll let anyone in the front door.

"You had no right to come here, and you had no right to call yourself my daddy," I insisted in a low, intense voice.

The eager grin left his face. "I know I'm doing this all wrong," he admitted. "I'm sorry, I—"

"What about that message I got that you would wait for my call, huh?" I asked him heatedly. "I thought it was supposed to be my decision whether or not to meet you."

"It was," Monroe agreed. "I guess I just couldn't wait."

"Well, too bad for you," I replied. I refused to let the hurt on his face get to me. "Look, would you just leave? I don't know you. I don't *want* to know you."

"Are you really that hard, child?" he asked me softly.

"Yes," I snapped. We stared at each other. I wouldn't give an inch.

"There's so much I want to say to you . . ." he began.

"As far as I know you had ten damn years to say whatever you wanted to me, so I don't see why you need to come interrupting my life now."

"All I'm asking for is a half hour of your time," Monroe said. "Give me that, and then if you want, I will get out of your life forever."

I felt so many things—sad, scared, and mad—all at once. Why should I spend even a half hour with him? Why should I let him in at all? But if I turned him away forever without that half hour, maybe I would always wonder what it was he wanted to say to me.

"Okay," I relented. "A half hour, and that's it."

"Great," he said, that grin lighting up his handsome face. "We can go for dinner, okay? When you finish your practice?"

"Coffee," I corrected him. "You can wait for me at Musical Burgers—it's on West End. I'll meet you there in about an hour."

"I'll be there, Sandy," he assured me.

"My name isn't Sandy," I said. "It's Sandra."

"Sandra," he repeated. "Okay. Your band sounds great, by the way."

Since I had vowed not to care what he thought, I didn't deign to reply. I just turned around to head back into rehearsal, and then I turned back to him. "One other thing. Don't you go around telling anyone in this town you're my daddy ever again. I have a daddy, and you're not him."

I didn't wait for his reaction, I just turned on my heel and walked away.

*　　*　　*

As soon as I walked into Musical Burgers, I saw him. He was sitting in a back booth, chatting with Bettina something-or-other, this waitress who wants to be a singer. They were deep in an animated conversation when I slid into the booth.

"You just hang in there, honey," my father was saying to her. "Don't no one make it overnight in the music business."

I winced at his grammar and shrugged off my jean jacket.

Bettina gave me a smile. "Your daddy is just fabulous," she told me sincerely. "I heard his *Been Down So Long It Looks like Up to Me* CD by the Monroe LaCrue Trio at my boyfriend Leeland's apartment—he's a major jazz fan. You must be so proud!"

I shot Monroe a cold look, which was lost on Bettina.

"Ya'll ready to order?" she asked us.

"Just coffee," I replied pointedly. "We won't be here long enough to eat."

"Make that two, sugar," Monroe said. Bettina scurried off.

"Didn't I just tell you an hour ago not to go telling people that you're my daddy?" I asked him.

"You did," he agreed. "I'm sorry. It's just

32

that I'm proud of you. Bettina said your band is getting quite a reputation around town."

"We're working hard," I said grudgingly. "What CD was she talking about?"

"I've got a new CD out on an independent label in Europe," Monroe explained. "We don't have an American distributor yet, so I was surprised that girl knew my work."

Bettina brought the coffee over, then shyly handed Monroe a sheet of notebook paper. "Would you mind signing this for my boyfriend?" she asked him. "Otherwise he'll never believe that I met you."

"My pleasure, baby," Monroe said, scribbling something on the paper.

I sipped my coffee and studied Monroe as he wrote. He was tall and well built, his skin a deeper brown than mine. He looked to be in his late thirties, and he really was handsome—almond-shaped eyes, a wide nose over a generous mouth. His hair was black, thick, and curly. He wore well-worn jeans and a denim shirt with the sleeves rolled up showing strong, young-looking arms. I couldn't help comparing his style to Larry's. Larry didn't own jeans or a denim shirt. In fact, I thought he might actually sleep in a three-piece suit. Then I felt disloyal, thinking that. So what if Larry was older and a little uptight and proper? He was the greatest father in the world, and he loved me.

As Monroe handed the paper back to Bettina and she scurried off, I ostentatiously looked at my watch. "You now have twenty-seven minutes left," I told him.

"You aren't making this easy."

"Good," I replied.

He sighed and sipped his coffee. "Let me tell you something about my life," he began. He stared into his coffee cup. "My people come from New Orleans—"

"I've heard," I said coolly.

"They've all passed on now," he continued, still looking into his coffee. "I always loved music, started playing jazz before I could talk. By the time I was a senior in high school I was playing with this jazz band at a tourist spot in the French Quarter—I lied about my age—and I figured school was just a waste of time. So I quit."

I nodded, waiting.

"I played around New Orleans for years. But you know, what seems like a lot of money when you're sixteen doesn't seem like so much when you get to be a man. I met your momma when she was singing backup behind Stevie Wonder at the Blue Note. She was so beautiful—I fell in love with her the instant I saw her. I mean to tell you I was lovesick, baby, as useless as a one-armed paperhanger."

I shot him a look of disdain. "I don't believe in love at first sight. That's ridiculous."

"No, it isn't, either," Monroe insisted. "I'm just sorry for you, if you haven't felt the wonder of it. She fell for me, too. Hard. Six weeks later we eloped."

"Mother Pearl still hasn't forgiven Mom for that," I said.

"I can understand," Monroe mused. "Your momma is her only daughter. So of course she wanted to see her have a big church wedding."

"And of course she wanted her to marry someone who hadn't dropped out of high school," I added.

"That's true," Monroe agreed. He took a sip of his coffee. "I followed your momma back to Detroit, figured I could do well there," he reminisced. "I heard there was a big jazz scene there." He looked at me. "It was good for a while. Your momma was doing a lot of backup work, I got a gig with a trio that played hotels. It didn't pay much, but at least I was working. Then you were born . . ."

"And I ruined everything in your little love nest, I suppose," I guessed.

"No, child, not at all," Monroe said. "We wanted you. And we both loved you with all our hearts. But . . . I was sad, see. And frustrated. There I was, playing all these standards every night to these folks who weren't even listening—you know—salesmen on the road trying to score on some lady, lonely wives laughing too loud. All cover tunes. No one would let me play my own music. So . . . I started to drink."

"Oh, yeah, here comes the sob story," I snorted.

"I started to drink," he repeated. "More and more. Then I'd do a few lines now and then because it made me feel better, I thought. Lines are—"

"Cocaine," I said. "Believe me, everyone over the age of ten knows what lines are."

He nodded. "Your momma and I started to grow apart. It was my fault. She was happy, singing behind other folks. She doesn't write her own stuff, and she never wanted to be no star. And she couldn't understand why I couldn't be satisfied . . ."

"Oh, that's a terrific reason to turn to drugs and alcohol," I said sarcastically. "That's a wonderful reason to break up a marriage and turn your back on your kid."

"I never said it was a good reason," Monroe said patiently. "I just said I would tell you the truth. Things got worse and worse. I spent more time getting high. In fact, I spent most of my money on blow. And finally your momma couldn't take it anymore. She said either I had to give up all that stuff or she would leave me. And . . . and I couldn't give it up."

"Because you're weak," I said, staring him dead in the eye.

"Yes, because I was weak," he agreed, staring right back at me. "But I'm not weak anymore. I went to Europe a couple of years after your momma and me broke up. My friend Barry—he plays trumpet—he told me to come over to France and play with him. He said they were color-blind over there. And you know I couldn't take this racist life here anymore, I really couldn't. There's no place for a black man in America today."

"That is a lot of bull," I seethed. "It's an excuse, because you didn't want to finish your education or work hard."

Monroe raised his eyebrows at me. "You don't believe America is a racist country?"

"Of course I do," I said. "I'm not blind and I'm not stupid. But it's also an excuse. No one told you to drop out of school or spend your money on drugs and alcohol. The way I hear it, you didn't grow up in some impoverished ghetto with no opportunities—"

"That's true," Monroe agreed. "My momma was a nurse, and my daddy was a factory foreman. But that doesn't mean a young black man who is a jazz musician doesn't have a real hard row to hoe in this country. I got twice the money and twice the respect when I left America."

I shrugged, unwilling to concede his point.

He sipped his coffee. "So, I went. And they do love jazz over there. But I drank my way through eight years of playing with Barry, so a lot of it's a big blur. See, I changed countries, but I didn't change my life. And then one day I knew I had to stop or I would die. I just hit bottom—that's what we call it in AA—Alcoholics Anonymous."

He looked into the distance as he remembered. "I got sober two years ago. I met a wonderful woman—she helped me. And I haven't touched a drop of liquor or a drug since then." He smiled. "After that, everything began to change. I started a new trio, and we got a deal—that's the CD the waitress was talking about. I'm finally playing my own tunes, Sandy—I mean Sandra." His eyes were shining. "And I knew I had to come find you, my child, my only child."

"Why?" I whispered.

He leaned toward me. "To make amends. To tell you that I've always loved you, and I'm so sorry I was never a daddy to you."

Tears blurred my vision. "How can you say you always loved me? You never called me, never wrote, never sent me even one stupid birthday card—"

"I know," he agreed. "I was wrong. So wrong. But I thought it was better. Try to understand. I hated myself. I didn't think I deserved to even have a daughter. And I kept telling myself you were better off without a loser like me."

"You were right," I sniffled, reaching into my purse for a Kleenex.

"No, I was wrong," he insisted, reaching for my hand. "I threw away your childhood, and I can never have that back. You don't know me, and I don't know you. But ... all I'm asking for is a chance, Sandra. To get to know you. To be a part of your life."

I pulled my hand away and blew my nose. "I just don't know," I gulped. "I'm all confused."

"I can understand that," he said quietly.

"Maybe we should just leave well enough

alone," I said. "Larry, my stepfather, he's a really great guy. He was always there for me, you know? He did all that dad stuff that you never did." I looked over at Monroe. "It'll hurt him if I spend time with you."

"I wouldn't ever try to take anything away from him—what he did for you," Monroe said earnestly.

I shredded the Kleenex between my fingers. "I feel . . . I feel so mad!" I blurted out. "You come waltzing into my life because you finally got your act together, and I'm just supposed to forgive and forget!"

"No, I don't expect you to do that," Monroe said quietly. He ran his finger over a crack in the table. "Maybe . . . could we spend some time together this week? Just a little time? You don't have to decide anything about me now. And if you decide at the end of the week you don't want me in your life, I'll respect that. Okay?"

"Okay." I couldn't believe I was agreeing, but the word came right out of my mouth without my thinking about it.

"I'm so glad, baby," he said fervently, reaching for my hand again.

I moved it away. "Look, stop calling me baby and honey and all that," I snapped. "I hate it."

"It's just my way of talking," he said gently.

"I know. That's what I hate. Those . . . those mindless endearments, so meaningless . . ."

"All right," he agreed. "I'll try not to do that. Now, can I take my daughter to dinner tomorrow night?"

I had tennis after school and a quick junior class officers' meeting, but otherwise I was free. We didn't have band practice because Jane had to work at her part-time job at Uncle Zap's, a music store at the mall.

"You can, on a couple of conditions," I said slowly. "One is I'll meet you wherever we're going. Two is don't call me your daughter."

"Okay," Monroe said. "There's a nice restaurant at my hotel. How about if we meet there at seven?"

I agreed.

Monroe paid the bill and we left. I wouldn't even shake his hand in front of the restaurant, I just told him a terse good-bye and headed for my Jeep.

On the way home I thought about what I'd decided. A part of me wanted to get to know him, and a part of me hated him too much to try.

And then there was Larry. How could I be so disloyal to Larry?

"Sandra? I'm in the kitchen," Larry called to me when he heard me come in the front door.

I found him making himself a huge sandwich on a roll. "I can only get away with this because your mother is at the recording studio late," he said, adding another dollop of mayonnaise to his creation. "Care to join me?"

"No, thanks," I said, and kissed him on the cheek. He was so sweet. His only weakness in life—besides my mother, whom he adores—is fatty foods. He has a cute round little belly that is usually hidden under a well-cut vest. At the moment it was clearly visible under his bathrobe.

"So how was band practice?" he asked, setting his plate on the kitchen table and sitting down.

"Good," I replied. I sat down with him. "We worked on stuff for the Battle of the Bands."

Larry took a huge bite of his sandwich. "This is fabulous," he said, his eyes closed in ecstasy. He washed down the sandwich with some milk. "Did you think any more about the situation with Monroe?" he asked me.

"Actually he . . ." I began, and then I stopped myself. I couldn't tell Larry the truth. I just couldn't. "He's been on my mind," I invented. "I'm definitely not going to see him."

Larry patted my hand. "That's probably for the best. Your mother and I discussed it earlier. We both think he'd only do you harm."

"I don't believe he'd do me anything," I said, getting up, "because I don't care about him. There's one thing I know, Lar, and that's when you don't care about someone, they absolutely cannot hurt you."

CHAPTER 4

Okay, this meeting is called to order," I said.

It was the next day after school, and I was not in a very good mood. Even though I'd really concentrated while taking some practice serves with my tennis coach, Avery Mandell, I'd kept making my toss too low so that I hit into the net. He was very ticked—he yelled at me in front of everyone else on the team, and then he stormed off to the locker room. I couldn't really fault him, either. I knew I hadn't been playing my best. We'd had a match with Hillsboro High the week before, and I had dropped a match I should have easily won.

Now I was at the junior class officers' meeting, and Jennie Neuman was giving me that stupid supercilious look of hers, as if to say "You don't deserve to be president of this class and everyone knows it."

"Jennie, do you have the minutes from the last meeting?" I asked her.

"Why, yes, Sandra, I do," Jennie said, opening her notebook. She was perched on the edge of a desk, her legs crossed at the ankles. She had on one of those flowery pale peach outfits with a lace collar and a matching hair bow tying back her long, glossy chestnut brown hair. She was perfectly groomed, down to her pale peach nail polish.

"At the last meeting we agreed to discuss whether junior class athletes whose grades fall below a C-plus average should be allowed to play in the homecoming football game," Jennie reported.

"Okay, we know there's a school rule about this," Dennis, the vice president of the class, said. "The blue book says that athletes can't play if they don't make their grades. But that rule has never been enforced in the history of this school."

"Then some kids protested," Jennie continued. "Someone started a petition, saying how hypocritical the school was, how they bend over backwards for athletes, especially football players. But the only kids who signed that stupid petition are losers—you know, the real geeks."

I ignored her last remark because it was too insipid to warrant a response. "Are the athletes held to a different standard?" I asked evenly, drumming my pencil on my desk.

"Yeah, if you mean lower," Tim Hershy, our class treasurer, replied. "See, this group that started the petition is mad because last year the kids in forensics whose grades fell below a C-plus average weren't allowed to go compete in this statewide competition in Memphis—"

"That's what I'm trying to tell ya'll," Jennie interrupted. "Losers and geeks."

"Jennie, you're supposed to be a class officer. Do you think you could attempt some level of maturity about this?" I asked her.

"In other words, stop being such a butt-head," Tim translated.

"Oh, calling me a butt-head is just *so* mature," Jennie drawled. "I am simply trying to make a point. Let's face it, everyone in this school is not equal."

"Yes, Jennie, they are," I replied coldly. "And it seems to me that the kids who signed this petition have a legitimate point."

"Well, excuse me, *Madam* President," Jennie said, "but I just don't think you understand."

"No? Well, then, maybe you'll enlighten me," I replied frostily.

"Of course," Jennie said sweetly. "Football is important to this school. Very important. The two guys who would be banned from playing are Kevin and Bryan, the first-string quarterback and the first-string fullback. It would be a total disaster! If we as class officers agree with these troublemakers, there will be all heck to pay!"

"Woah, Jennie said 'heck,' " Dennis teased. "Somebody wash out her mouth!"

"I happen to know there's another petition goin' around," Jennie drawled. "In favor of the athletes. I happen to have a copy right here."

"Why, how convenient," I told her. She handed me a few sheets of paper stapled together, and I scanned them quickly, noting that the petition was signed first by the football team and by Katie Lynn Kilroy and none other than Jennie Neuman herself.

Katie Lynn and Jennie were best friends. They both had boyfriends on the football team. They were both in that clique of girls who thought they should run the school and dictate everyone's life—you know, arbiters of both taste and morals. Jane calls them the pastel people.

My last run-in with them had been when they started something called Teens for Righteousness, a right-wing group hiding under the guise of being "good Christians," who believed in banning certain books. Yeah, certain books, like *Tom Sawyer* and *One Flew Over the Cuckoo's Nest* and *Soul on Ice*—anything they found offensive. It didn't matter if it was great literature. So far we had managed to keep them from banning any books at Green Hills High, but it was a major struggle.

"I notice your name and Katie Lynn's name are on the top of this petition," I said.

Jennie nodded. "That's what I mean. Look at the other petition. I mean, kids like Dinah Fairweather and Betsy Winters and Jane McVay signed it, for pity's sake!"

"What is your point, Jennie?" I asked, my eyes narrowing. I could practically feel the steam coming out of my ears, I was so mad, but she paid no attention.

"My point is that these kids are total zeros! Dinah has buckteeth and she lives in some kind of shack or something, I hear, and Betsy Winters must weigh two hundred pounds, and

Jane McVay, well, everyone knows she's doing it with just about every guy in the junior class!"

I stood up, my hands clenched into fists. "That is a lie and you know it," I said in a low voice.

"Well, I know she's in your little band and all," Jennie said blithely, "but you should know what everyone is saying!"

"I don't care what you and your ignorant friends are saying, Jennie," I seethed, advancing on her slowly. "But I am telling you this. If you go spreading any more ugly lies about Jane, I will personally see that you live to regret it, have you got that?"

"Hey, hey," Dennis said, stepping between us. "Let's chill out here, ladies."

Jennie sat back down on the desk. "I'm fine," she said coolly. "I am, however, making a note that the president of the junior class threatened me and my friends." She wrote briskly in her notebook.

I really, truly wanted to kill her.

"Let's get back to the petitions, okay?" Tim suggested.

"Fine," I said, using all my self-control. "The way I see it, it doesn't matter how important football is. Fair is fair. Either the rule should be abolished or the guys whose grades fell don't get to play in the homecoming football game."

Jennie looked around at Dennis and Tim. "Do ya'll agree with that?"

"Absolutely," Dennis said firmly.

"It's gotta be fair," Tim said with a shrug.

Jennie slid off the desk. "Well, I don't think you people realize what you're getting into with that decision."

"I think we can live with the consequences," I said dryly. "Besides, all we're doing is giving our recommendation as class officers. We don't make the rules here."

"Fine," Jennie said primly. "But when I write up the report on this and turn it in to the administration, I intend to make sure it says I was in total disagreement with ya'll. And I guess the mayor—who I might remind you always comes to homecoming because he's an alumnus of this high school—will be interested in what you have to say. He expects us to win, you know. Everyone expects us to win. And without Kevin Jarvis and Bryan Phillips, we might just as well let Hillsboro High celebrate their victory now."

"Well, I guess Kevin and Bryan should have thought about that before they let their grades drop so low," I replied.

Jennie sighed and brushed past me, leaning close. She whispered so low that I was sure Dennis and Tim couldn't hear. "Your days are numbered," she said, and she walked out the door.

"She's a piece of work," I muttered, gathering up my books.

"Ignore her," Dennis advised easily. "She's not interesting enough to take seriously."

"She calls herself a Christian," I said, shaking my head ruefully. "She is so far from being a Christian . . ."

Dennis put his arm around my shoulders and gave me a little hug. "I'm telling you, Sandra, don't let her get to you. That's just what she wants, and then she wins."

"I'd like to make voodoo dolls of her and all her self-righteous little friends and stick pins in them."

"You?" Tim laughed. "Pragmatic Sandra? I thought you were above all their petty nonsense!"

I sighed. "You're right. But that witch has been getting to me lately, she really has."

"Hey," Dennis said, "I refuse to spend another second on the subject of Jennie—like I said, she ain't worth it. Now, ya'll want to go get something to eat?"

"I'm in," Tim said.

"Sorry, I have to run," I told Dennis.

"You always have to run," he grumbled good-naturedly. "You are the busiest human I ever knew."

He looked disappointed. I kind of sort of thought he might like me as more than a friend. I liked him, too. He was about my height, with curly blond hair and nice warm brown eyes. He was smart and funny, and unlike Darryl, Dennis was very easygoing and laid back.

Sometimes I'd catch Dennis looking at me in that certain way, that you're-a-girl-I-could-seriously-like way. But I never followed up on those looks. I mean, Darryl and I had been a couple forever—everyone knew that, even Dennis. Still, if I was free ... but I wasn't. So I was happy to have Dennis as a good buddy.

I kissed him on the cheek. "I'll take a rain check," I promised, and hurried out the door.

And ran smack into Darryl.

"Well, hi there," I said with surprise, my face burning. I felt guilty that I'd even been *thinking* about another guy.

"For you," Darryl said, bringing a single red rose out from behind his back.

"That's so sweet," I said, and I meant it. I took the rose and wrapped my arms around his neck, loving the feel of being in his arms. "God, it's so good to see you," I murmured into his neck. "I have been having the most rotten day."

"Want to talk about it?" Darryl asked.

"No, I want to forget about it." I kissed him lightly. "So, what are we celebrating? And how did you know where to find me?"

"What we're celebrating is that I finished that monster research paper on the autoimmune system, and how I found you is I went by your place and your mom told me you were still at school." He wrapped his arm around my shoulders and we walked toward my Jeep. Want to go do something fun?"

I looked at my watch. "I'd love to," I replied, "but I have to be somewhere in two hours, and I have to shower and change first."

Darryl raised his eyebrows. "Shower and change for band practice?"

"This is something else," I hedged. "Hey, how about we go for a drive? And take a walk by the lake?"

"Sounds great," Darryl agreed. "Let's take your Jeep—it's a lot nicer than my ancient bomb."

I handed him my car keys—he loves to drive my Jeep—and we drove out toward Hendersonville, the windows open to let in the still-warm autumn air.

"Mmmm, this is great," I said, letting my head fall back on the seat. "This is the first chance I've had to relax all day." I closed my eyes, and the next thing I knew the Jeep was stopped and Darryl's lips were on my neck.

"Mmmm? What?" I mumbled, sitting up.

"You fell asleep," Darryl said tenderly, rubbing his knuckles gently over my cheek.

"Oh, God, what time is it?" I asked frantically, looking at my watch.

"It's okay, we've only been here a few minutes," Darryl assured me. He smiled. "You looked so pretty asleep like that." He leaned over and gave me the sweetest, softest kiss. I put my arms around his neck and kissed him back. It was delicious.

"You know what I think about sometimes?" he murmured. "I think about you and me and this great house we're gonna have. And our medical practice. A couple of rug rats running around the house. And getting to wake up to your face every single morning."

"That is so nice," I said softly.

"And I think about sleeping next to you

every single night," Darryl continued in his deep, sexy voice. "All you're wearing is the top to my pajamas . . ."

"Is that so?" I asked in a teasing voice.

"It is," he agreed somberly. "And I get to take that pajama top off of you very slowly, every single night." His hand toyed with the top button of my shirt.

"Don't get carried away," I said with a laugh, playfully slapping his hand away. "I can't stay that long."

"Oh, that's right, you've got to be somewhere," Darryl remembered. He leaned over to kiss me again, and the kiss escalated until we were both breathless.

"I have a feeling you're trying to get me to forget my appointment," I whispered.

"Would I do a thing like that?" He kissed my cheek, my ear, then he nuzzled my neck. "So, what is this big appointment?"

I hadn't planned to tell Darryl the truth, I really hadn't. Oh, he knew that Larry wasn't my birth father, and he knew I had a birth father out there somewhere. But he also knew that my birth father was, according to my mother, and I quote, "a-no-good-two-timing-low-life-no-account-raggedy-ass-loser," end quote. I mean, even as my mother had told me to make my own decision about seeing my father, I knew she really didn't want me to have anything to do with him.

But just at the moment I felt so close to Darryl and he was being so loving, that . . . well, I just blurted out the truth.

"You're *what?*" he asked in shock.

"Having dinner with my birth father," I repeated. I gave him a short version of the story to date, then I took his hand and waited for his reaction.

"So you're telling me he just showed up here?" Darryl asked.

I nodded.

"And you're going to have dinner with him."

I nodded again.

"Excuse me, Sandra, but have you lost your mind?"

I dropped his hand. "I don't think so," I said evenly.

"Why would you want to let this loser into your life?" Darryl asked me incredulously.

"He's my father—" I began.

"Oh bull," Darryl exploded. "Lawrence is your father, that's what you always say."

"Of course, but—"

"But nothing," Darryl said. "I'll tell you

what you should do. You should tell this fool to go back to wherever the hell he came from—"

"Why? Because you say so?" I asked heatedly.

"No, because you have a brain!" Darryl replied. "What, you think he wants to be your daddy all of a sudden?"

"No," I replied defensively. "He just wants to get to know me, he said . . ."

Darryl sighed. "Sandra, this is the man who walked out on you and your momma. This is the man who never, ever found the time to call you or write you or send one thin dime to help support you. He's an alcoholic and a drug addict—"

"He was. He isn't now."

"What, are you defending him now?" Darryl asked me, his voice rising.

"No, I'm just trying to explain—"

"Sandra, baby, this guy is out to use you for something. That's what I think," Darryl said intensely. "And here you are, too busy to do all the things you have to do as it is, and you want to let this no-account fool into your life to mess you up even more?"

"All I'm doing is having dinner with him!" I yelled. "God, I'm sorry I even told you!"

We sat there, breathing hard at each other, not saying a word.

"Look, just take me back to school so you can get your car," I finally said.

"Fine," Darryl replied tersely, and he turned on the ignition.

We drove in silence, both of us too mad to talk. He pulled my Jeep up next to his car, shut it off, and turned to me. "Look, maybe I overreacted."

"No kidding," I muttered.

"I just don't want him to hurt you," Darryl said softly.

"I don't think you should judge someone you don't even know," I told him, taking my car keys from him.

Darryl got out of the Jeep and stuck his head back in. "I know everything about a guy like him that I need to know, Sandra."

"Well, maybe I don't," I replied. "Maybe there's all kinds of things about him I need to know."

"You don't need him, baby," Darryl said earnestly. "I love you, and I'll take care of you. I'll always take care of you."

Those words felt like a noose around my neck. How could I love Darryl so much and want to pull away from him so much, both at the same time?

"I love you, too," I finally said, "but I don't want either one of you to take care of me, Darryl. I want to take care of myself."

Then I started my Jeep, and I drove away.

CHAPTER
5

♡

*Y*ou look lovely," Monroe said as I walked over to the table near the window where he was already seated, waiting for me. He quickly got up and held my chair.

"Thanks," I said, and sat down. I noticed he was dressed up, wearing a really nice double-breasted olive green suit and a gold silk shirt. I had tried on and discarded half the clothes in my closet before forcing myself to settle on a pair of wide-legged black crepe pants and a white poet's blouse with ruffly sleeves.

I settled into my chair and looked around. It was a nice place—plush forest green chairs and carpet, pristine white tablecloths, soft lighting, tuxedoed waiters moving discreetly around the room. I turned back to Monroe and noticed him sipping orange liquid from a glass.

"A screwdriver?" I asked with disgust.

"Orange juice and seltzer," he corrected me with a smile. "What would you like?"

The waiter appeared at our table. "Tomato juice, please," I told him. I turned back to Monroe. "So . . ."

He raised his eyebrows. "So?"

"You wanted me to come, I'm here," I said tersely.

"I see that," he said. He sipped his drink. "You can relax, you know. No one is going to bite you, honey. You look like you're about to catapult yourself out of that seat any second."

I scowled. "I am relaxed," I lied. "And don't call me honey."

Sure. How could I possibly be relaxed? I had messed up at tennis, the secretary of the junior class was out to get me, I'd had a fight with my boyfriend, and then I had lied to my parents and told them I was going to see a play at Vanderbilt.

"Have you ever been here before?" Monroe asked me.

I shook my head no.

"I heard there's a good jazz trio that comes

on in a few minutes," he said, cocking his head toward a small stage in the far corner of the room. "At least that's what they told me at the front desk."

"Great," I replied in a flat voice. I picked up the menu and scanned it quickly, then put it down. I felt awful—jumpy and guilty and . . . just awful. "Look," I told Monroe. "This isn't working. I shouldn't have come here."

He looked stricken. "Don't say that."

"I'm sorry, but I can't do this," I said. "I lied to my parents about where I was going, I have tons of homework to do, and . . . I just have to go." I started to get up.

"Please," Monroe said, quickly standing and grabbing my arm. "Please."

The waiter came over with my tomato juice. "Is something wrong?" he asked solicitously.

"No, nothing," I murmured, and sat back down. "Look, I'll compromise with you," I said in a low voice. "We'll drink this, and we'll make inane chitchat, and then I'll go. We'll skip dinner. How's that?"

He stared at me carefully. "All right," he finally agreed. "You call the shots."

I sipped my tomato juice. "So," I said, "tell me about your life or something."

He gave me a small smile. "My life. Well, it's a hell of a lot better than it used to be."

"What's going on with your jazz trio while you're here playing long-lost father with me?" I asked him.

"Actually, we're on a three-week break while Johann—he's my bass player—is recuperating from tendonitis. Then we'll be touring Scandinavia."

"Glad I could work so conveniently into your schedule," I said.

"It wasn't convenience that brought me here, Sandra," Monroe said. "I've been thinking about it for a long time. My lady friend, Marie, she helped me decide to just do it, just come on and try to see you."

"Is this the same lady friend who helped you get straight?"

He nodded. "She's a wonderful woman. I'd like for you to meet her sometime."

"So, if she's so wonderful why don't you marry her?" I asked.

"I plan on it," he replied. "But I promised Marie and my AA sponsor I'd be two years clean and sober before I proposed. I have another two months to go."

I fiddled with the little straw in my drink. "What does this Marie person do?"

"She's a physical therapist in Paris," he explained, his eyes lighting up. "I met her when

I went to this hospital for sick kids—I played for some benefit. It's kind of a blur, since I was drunk most of the time back then."

"She's into drunks?" I asked dryly.

"Well, let's just say she knows a lot about them, since both her parents died of alcoholism," he explained. "If it wasn't for Marie, I don't believe I'd be sitting here today."

"A saint, huh?"

"Something like that," he agreed with a grin. "Here, I'll show you her picture." He reached into his back pocket and pulled out his wallet, flipping it open to a small photo of him with his arm around a pretty white woman with a halo of frizzy brown hair.

"She's white," I noted.

"Is that a problem?" he asked with surprise.

I shrugged, but I felt funny. It's not that I cared—Mom and Lawrence had raised me to be proud I'm African American, and color-blind in judging people—but there was something about knowing Monroe's great savior was a great *white* savior that felt like even more of a rejection of me and my mother. I couldn't tell him that, though.

I was about to hand the wallet back to him when the photo opposite caught my eye. I pulled it to me and looked closely. It was a photo of Monroe and my mom, both very young and happy-looking, and toddler me in a white frilly dress standing holding on to both of their hands. I looked over at Monroe.

"I've always carried that photo," he said softly.

I handed him back his wallet wordlessly.

"You were such a happy little thing," Monroe reminisced. "Always singing and dancing around. And bossy! You always knew better."

"Did I?" I asked.

"Yes, ma'am. I always said you were born to run the world. Independent, too. Couldn't no one tell you nothing. You had to do things yourself. I remember you wanted to learn to roller-skate because this big girl down the street could roller-skate. So we got you some skates, and I tried to hold your hand but you waved me off. Boom, you fell down, over and over, but you always got right back up. You never cried. And you wouldn't let me help you—"

"Excuse me, aren't you Monroe LaCrue?" a low voice asked.

I looked up. A white guy in his thirties with his blond hair swept back into a ponytail was standing there, an eager look on his face.

"Yes," Monroe said.

"Ed Hamon," the man said eagerly, sticking out his hand to shake Monroe's. "My quartet is just about to go on—the Ed Hamon Group—and I said to my drummer, Pete, 'Dang if that isn't Monroe LaCrue sittin' at that table.'"

Monroe smiled. "It's nice to be recognized, thanks."

"Well, raise my rent!" Ed crowed. "Monroe LaCrue. You are one of my all-time idols, I don't mind sayin'! I bummed around Europe several years ago and heard you play in this little dive in Paris, somewhere near the Sorbonne—I forget the name. You played that piano so sweet—man, I fell in love with that sound. I had been a hard-core rocker, but when I heard you play, I just fell in love with jazz, and I been playin' it ever since."

"Thanks for the compliment," Monroe said. "I appreciate it."

"I even remember the name of this one tune you did—'Lost Child.' You wrote that, right?"

Monroe nodded.

"That tune haunted me, man. I couldn't get it out of my head. I was always asking other musicians, 'You ever heard this tune "Lost Child"?' No one knew it. Then when I was in Germany last month I saw this CD at my buddy's house, and there you were—the Monroe LaCrue Trio! I popped that baby in and listened. First cut, first side—'Lost Child.' I couldn't believe it. It blew me away, man."

"Thanks," Monroe said.

"So, what's a jazz man like you doin' here in the heart of country-music country?" Ed asked.

"Visiting my daughter," Monroe said, nodding at me. "Sandra LaCrue."

I winced. I didn't consider myself his daughter, and my last name wasn't LaCrue, thank-you-very-much, but no one seemed to notice my irritation.

"It's a real pleasure," Ed said, pumping my hand. "Your father is awesome."

"Sandra's a musician, too," Monroe said. "She has a band called Wild Hearts."

"No kidding?" Ed marveled. "You inherited your old man's talent, huh?"

"My mother is a musician, too," I replied.

"Wow, talented family!" Ed exclaimed. He turned back to Monroe. "Hey, is there any chance in this world I could get you up to do a number?"

"Oh, no," Monroe demurred, "I'm here with my daughter—"

"I can't tell you how much it would mean

67

to me," Ed continued. "How about 'Lost Child'? The guys know it—they've all heard your CD."

Monroe looked over at me.

Frankly, I was curious to hear him perform. "Go on," I encouraged him. "I'd like to hear you."

"Well . . . all right, then," Monroe said, standing up.

"Incredible!" Ed exclaimed. "The guys are gonna be major-league psyched to play with you."

"Excuse me," Monroe said to me, and he headed off to the stage with Ed.

Monroe sat down at the piano, and Ed quickly conferred with the other three musicians. I saw them all nod eagerly, then go over to shake Monroe's hand. Then Ed went to the microphone.

"Ladies and gentlemen, if I could have your attention, please. We're the Ed Hamon Group. I'm Ed Hamon, and I've got a real treat for ya'll tonight. Sitting in with us is a man who has been one of my musical inspirations. All the way from Paris, France, please welcome Mr. Monroe LaCrue!"

Some people clapped lightly—clearly no one in the restaurant had heard of Monroe except the musicians, but southerners are very polite.

"Thank you," Monroe said into his vocal mike. "This is a tune I wrote for my daughter, Sandra. It's called 'Lost Child.' "

He played a long, twinkly run on the piano, then nodded into the downbeat and the other musicians came in. The melody was mournful, full of minor chords, the music languid and soulful. Then Monroe leaned into his vocal mike and began to sing.

Seems like just yesterday
I saw your smile
Even though I know
I haven't seen it for the longest while.

Seems like forever
Till I can explain
How I could have up and gone
And caused you such pain.

Seems like I'll never
Have the chance to say
All the things I meant to tell you
When I went away.

Seems like you'll never
Know how I care
That in my dreams I see you
Everywhere.

> But I lost you, child,
> Child of my own,
> Lost Child,
> Where have you gone?

I could hardly see the stage because I was looking through a veil of tears. The salty liquid ran into my mouth. I didn't care. He was singing about me. He had written that song about me. And he had written it a long time ago—because it was years ago when Ed Hamon heard him sing it in Paris. I thought my daddy had completely forgotten about me, never gave me a single thought, had discarded me like some old rag.

But it wasn't true. It wasn't.

> But I lost you, child,
> Child of my own,
> Lost Child,
> Where have you gone?
>
> Sweet Lost Child,
> Where have you gone?

When the song was done, everyone in the restaurant applauded enthusiastically.

As for me, well, I guess I applauded hardest of all.

Monroe came back to the table. I stood up. We looked at each other, and the next thing I knew I was in his arms.

"Why didn't you ever tell me? Why didn't you ever call me?" I gasped between sobs.

"I didn't deserve you," he whispered into my hair. "I'm so, so sorry, Sandra. But I'm here now. And I'll never, ever be gone from your life again."

I pulled away, terribly embarrassed. Everyone in the restaurant seemed to be staring at us.

I wiped my hand across my face. "I must be a mess," I sniffled.

"You're beautiful," Monroe insisted. He handed me his gold silk hanky and I blew my nose. "I'll get this washed for you," I promised, sitting back down.

He sat, too. "It's not important." He reached over and cupped my hands in his. "Now can we have dinner and really start to get to know each other? Please?"

"Yes," I replied. "Yes, we can."

And that's exactly what we did.

CHAPTER
6

⟨♡⟩

We heard a rapping at the slightly open door of the Leemans' music room.

"You girls ready for a break?" Gramma Beth called from outside the music room as we were talking about the song—one of the originals by Jane—that we had just finished rehearsing. Savy was telling Kimmy that she had to speed up the guitar lick she added at the bridge, and Kimmy was getting that embarrassed look on her face that she always gets when she thinks she hasn't done something right.

"Sure!" Savy called out to her grandmother, turning her attention away from Kimmy. "Come on in."

It was the Thursday evening before the Battle of the Bands at Vanderbilt, and we were having our last official rehearsal. We'd been at it since six-thirty, and it was already nine-thirty. I'd told my parents that I'd be home by eleven. Larry wasn't very happy that I was out so late on a school night, but I'd managed to convince him that this was a life-or-death situation—in other words, if I didn't stay through the whole rehearsal, the other girls in Wild Hearts would kill me.

"Hi, ya'll," Gramma Beth said as she came into the room carrying a tray with what looked like homemade cookies and four glasses of milk. "Ya'll sound great. But I think the guitar part on the bridge could be faster."

"I knew it," Kimmy groaned, burying her head in her hands, but the rest of us cracked up.

"That's just what I said!" Savy exclaimed, jumping to her feet to take the tray from Gramma Beth. "Kimmy'll speed it up next time—right, Kimmy?"

"Right," Kimmy said meekly. "Sorry."

"I think we should dock you or something every time you apologize," I suggested, reaching for a glass of milk.

"Dock her what?" Jane asked. "We aren't making any money."

"If we win the Battle of the Bands, we win a thousand dollars," Savy reminded us.

"And if donkeys had wings, they could fly," I replied.

"You just watch that negative thinking," Gramma Beth scolded me, taking a seat on the couch and folding her arms.

"Yes, ma'am," I replied. I snuck a look over at her. I didn't want to say anything about it, but the fact was, she looked terrible. Sick, even. She was moving slowly—usually she was a ball of fire, just like Savy. There were dark circles under her eyes. Even her glorious red hair looked duller and thinner.

I glanced over at Savy and saw concern etched on her face. She took a seat next to Gramma Beth and hugged her gently. "It's so great that you're up! You look so much better!"

Gramma Beth arched an eyebrow at Savy. "Better than what?"

"Better than . . . before!" Savy exclaimed. "Thanks for the snack. Now, don't you think you should go rest?"

"You hush, child," Gramma Beth replied, her voice slightly less firm than usual. "There's just so long a body can stay horizontal before it petrifies!"

We all laughed a little too loud. I, for one, hated to hear this incredible, feisty woman even joke about petrifying.

"We're so glad you're out of the hospital," Kimmy said in her soft voice.

"Not half as glad as I am!" Gramma Beth replied, getting up from the couch. It hurt my heart to see how difficult it was for her. "Well, I have a million things to do, so I better get," she said, heading for the door. Then she turned back to us. "And I'll be listening, Kimmy Carrier, so speed up that bridge!"

We all laughed nervously again as Gramma Beth gave us a wave and left the room.

"I gotta tell ya," Jane said from her perch behind her drum kit. "She doesn't look so good."

"She's fine," Savy insisted. "Nothing can beat her, you know?"

We all nodded, but I don't think any of us were convinced, not even Savy.

"My great-aunt Edith had a brain tumor," Kimmy said, nibbling at the edge of a cookie. "She got better."

"Oh! So, cool!" Jane cried, with forced gaiety in her voice.

Savy sighed and threw herself back on the couch. "Okay, I admit it," she said in a low voice. "I'm scared. Really scared." She looked up at us. "It's just . . . I can't imagine my life without her, you know?"

For some reason that made me think about Monroe—which was crazy, because I hadn't had him in my life at all until a few days before. But now that he was there, I couldn't imagine him not being there. It didn't make any sense, but there it was anyway.

"I always act really upbeat in front of Gramma Beth," Savy continued earnestly. "I don't want her to know how scared I am. And I do the same thing in front of my brothers and my sister. And with my parents it's even worse. It's like I feel as if I have to comfort them or something! It's crazy! So there's no one I can tell the truth to!"

"Us," Kimmy said softly.

Savy smiled. "Yeah, that's true."

Yowza, could I ever relate. I was lying to my parents about Monroe, and Darryl definitely didn't understand, so who could I talk to? Savy, Jane, and Kimmy, that's who.

If only I could get up the nerve.

I am not the kind of person who enjoys easy confidences. I like to believe I can handle everything myself. It's just my stupid pride, I suppose.

I looked at my watch—nine forty-five. And I'd planned with Monroe that he would bring the charts to "Lost Child" over to me at band practice around ten. I had planned to keep telling everyone that he was a friend of the family. But maybe, just maybe, I was ready to risk telling them the truth.

Except that for once in my life I had no idea how to say what I wanted to say. So I did the logical thing.

I stalled.

"Uh," I began. "I, uh . . ."

Jane laughed and reached for a cookie. "Uh? Did I just hear the indecisive sound of 'uh' pass your lips? What does 'uh' mean?"

"It means I have something to tell you," I replied, nervously biting the inside of my lip.

"You're pregnant," Jane guessed.

"Not hardly," I said dryly. "Darryl and I are fighting. Besides, I wouldn't be that stupid."

"So?" Jane asked, taking a big swig of milk. "What's up?"

"Well," I began, "you know that friend of the family who stopped by rehearsal the other night?"

"Great-looking, for an older guy," Jane said. "You acted very weird when he was here." Her face lit up. "Oh, God, are you dating him behind Darryl's back?"

I had to laugh at that. "No. And he's not a friend of the family, either. He *is* family."

They all looked at me quizzically.

"You've heard me talk about Larry.... Well, he's actually my stepfather," I explained. "And the man you met the other night is ... he's my father. My birth father." I quickly explained about how my father had been in Europe all these years. "His name is Monroe LaCrue," I finished. "He's a jazz musician."

Jane's mouth fell open. "Your father is Monroe LaCrue?" she asked me. "*The* Monroe LaCrue?"

"You know him?" I queried. I was sure that Jane had him mixed up with someone else.

"Who is he?" Savy asked.

"Who *is* he?" Jane echoed. "Only one of the best jazz pianists I've ever heard. He's better than McCoy Tyner!"

"Who's McCoy Tyner?" Kimmy wondered.

"Hey, I thought you only listened to rock," Savy said. "Since when do you know jazz?"

"Please, I'm from Manhattan," Jane replied huffily. "Everyone there knows jazz." She grinned. "Actually, I had a jazz technique class at the High School of Performing Arts last year," she admitted. "The teacher was this total jazz fanatic who had us listen to a demo of Monroe LaCrue. I swear to God I still remember how awesome it was!"

Kimmy turned to me, her eyes wide. "And he's your father?"

"Monroe LaCrue!" Jane crowed. "I can't believe it!"

"Believe it," I confirmed.

"But how did he end up in Nashville?" Savy said. "That is so amazing!"

"He came to meet me," I admitted.

Savy cocked her head to one side. "You mean you didn't know your own father?"

"I knew he existed," I said. "But once he left for Europe—I was about six or something—I never saw or heard from him again."

Compassion suffused Kimmy's face. "That's horrible," she said. "You must have felt terrible."

"I guess," I admitted. "I don't know. I don't remember much. I . . . I kind of hardened my heart to him."

"But why didn't he contact you all those years?" Savy asked me.

It was hard, but I told them the truth. About my parent's marriage. About Monroe's problems with drugs and alcohol. About how he claimed he had changed.

"Wow," Kimmy breathed. "So how do you feel now?"

"Confused," I admitted. "At first I didn't want to have anything to do with him. But then I started liking him. And now . . . now I feel guilty. Like if I see him, if I care for him, I'm being disloyal to my mom and to Larry. I'm just totally conflicted!"

"Let me put it to you this way," Jane said. "My father, a perfectly nice man, spends his days deciding the color of car interiors. Your father is Monroe LaCrue, a jazz great, and you're conflicted about whether to see him? Gimme a break!"

"Hey, it's not that simple," Savy said. "I understand."

"Me too," Kimmy agreed. "You want to know where he was all those years, right?"

I nodded. "No one forced him to do drugs or to be a drunk," I said. "It seems like a lousy, self-serving excuse."

"Hey, alcoholism is a disease," Jane said. "Anyway, that was then, this is now. You're both musicians! Think about how much you have in common!"

"Yes, I know," I replied. "And I know how he apologized to me. But I also hear this little voice in my head saying 'He didn't care about you. If he'd cared, he would have done something about it.' "

"He cares now," Savy pointed out. "He came all this way because he cares."

"Maybe," I allowed, nervously twisting a ring around and around on my finger. "But how do I know he's not doing all this to make himself feel better?"

"So what if that's part of it?" Jane asked. "Would that be so bad?"

"I don't know, I just don't know!" I exclaimed. "And I'm so busy—I can't get everything done as it is. He . . . he doesn't fit into my life!"

"Hey, Sandra, that's just the way life goes, you know?" Jane said.

I stared at the rag rug under my feet and then looked back up. "I guess . . . I guess what I'm most afraid of is that I'll let him in and I'll care and he'll burn me again." I got a lump in my throat. "I don't think I could take that."

"Maybe that's just a chance you'll have to take," Jane said matter-of-factly. "Because if you don't, you'll be rejecting him just like he rejected you."

"It's not the same," I argued.

"Close enough," Jane said with a shrug.

"All I know," Kimmy said quietly, "is that my parents are divorced from each other, but I usually feel like they divorced me, too. Neither of them pays any real mind to me at all. They don't have a clue about me—except to say that I disappoint them, which I suppose I do."

"So what are you saying?" I asked her.

"I'm saying," Kimmy said earnestly, "that I wouldn't mind if one of them apologized to me and then tried to really get to know me." She gave me a wan smile. "It's never going to happen in this lifetime, but it would be nice."

I smiled at Kimmy. So what if she was rich and fine-looking? She really didn't have it so great. "I see your point.

"My parents are totally against me having anything to do with Monroe," I continued. "In fact, I lied to them and told them I wasn't going to see him."

Savy shrugged. "You don't have to tell your parents everything."

"I know that," I agreed, "but I hate lying to them. And Darryl—I told him I was going to see Monroe, and he gave me this whole lecture about how stupid it was. We had a big fight."

"Darryl doesn't run your life," Jane said. "I mean, you told us he's even against the band— he thinks it's a waste of your time. That doesn't mean you're going to quit the band, right?"

"Right!" I said emphatically.

"So," Jane continued, "just because your parents say 'Jump,' that doesn't mean you have to answer 'How high?' "

Just then Savy's brother Dustin knocked at the music room door and stuck his head inside. He and his identical twin brother, Dylan, are both twenty years old and students at Vanderbilt. Dustin had recently gotten his hair cut short, while Dylan's was still long, which was the only way I could tell them apart.

"Sandra?" he asked. "There's someone here to see you. He says he's a friend of your family."

I looked around at my friends, and then I made a decision. "Tell my father to come in," I said.

Dustin looked confused. "Your father?" he asked. "He said he was—"

"My father," I repeated firmly.

Savy, Jane, and Kimmy gave me encouraging smiles and thumbs-up gestures, and then Monroe LaCrue was standing at the door of the music room.

"Savy, Kimmy, Jane," I said, "I'd like you to meet Monroe LaCrue, my father."

Monroe stared at me, his face proud, happy, and grateful. He didn't say a word.

It was Jane, per usual, who broke the silence.

"Mr. LaCrue?" she asked.

"Please, honey, call me Monroe," he said with a wide grin.

"Can you autograph Savy's piano for her?" Jane queried, a big grin on her face. "She's too shy to ask you herself."

Monroe only stayed at band practice a little while. We ran through "It Wasn't God Who Made Honky Tonk Angels" for him, and while he did say that he wasn't much into country music, he also said our harmony work was a thing of beauty.

I asked him to do "Lost Child" for us, and he did. It was so beautiful—even Jane had tears in her eyes. I felt so proud and so happy. That was my father. And he'd written that song about me.

We made plans for Monroe to come hear us play at the Battle of the Bands, and then he left. Practice broke up shortly after that. I wasn't looking forward to the rest of the night. I had about an hour of chemistry problems still to do, and there was no way I was getting to sleep before midnight. And then there was Mom and Larry, and facing them, knowing I was telling them lies.

Well, maybe I'd get lucky and they'd be in bed already.

I drove home and almost hit an opossum on Belmont Park Terrace as I pulled into our driveway. When I came in the front door, I heard voices in the living room.

Which meant I wasn't going to get lucky.

I walked into the living room, and there was Larry with my mom and Darryl.

This was not unusual. Darryl and I had been together so long that he was like part of the family. And he knew that I had chem homework to do, so probably he'd stopped by to help me with it. That would be just like him. No fight between us could be more important than my getting good grades.

And then a terrible thought hit me: he knew I had gone out with Monroe the night before, but my parents didn't. And I desperately didn't want Darryl to tell them.

He wouldn't. Would he?

"Hi!" I said as I breezed into the living room. "I'm not late, am I?"

"Not a bit," my mother said. "Right on time."

"Hey, sweetheart," Larry said. "We've just been chatting with Darryl."

My heart skipped a beat.

I looked at him, pleading with my eyes: You didn't tell them, did you? But I got no sense from him if he did or didn't.

"About what?" I asked nonchalantly. "Anything important?"

"P-chem," Darryl answered. "A course you're going to have to take for pre-med. I'm acing it, but it's killing me."

Thank God, I said to myself. He'd kept his mouth shut.

And then I wondered, For how long?

CHAPTER 7

♡

Ms. Cavelli, my eleventh grade honors English teacher, glanced at her watch and then closed the copy of Mark Twain's *Huckleberry Finn* that she'd been referring to constantly during class.

I knew what was coming, and I unconsciously crossed my fingers. It was Friday, the day before the Battle of the Bands, and Ms. Cavelli always gave back any papers or tests that she'd graded during the week at the end of class on Friday. We'd been discussing black writers in America, and two weeks before, we had turned in our last paper. The assignment had been to write a five-page paper on a book by any black American writer we wanted. I saw Ms. Cavelli pick up a pile of papers from her desk—clearly she was about to return those papers.

I'd picked a book that Larry had recommended to me, *Manchild in the Promised Land* by Claude Brown. It was written in the 1960s, Larry had told me, and it was the story of one man's struggle to get out of an inner-city ghetto.

Unfortunately, because of everything I was doing, I'd only had time to skim it, though it seemed like it was really great. That wasn't like me, not at all. I had intended to read the whole thing, but somehow . . . somehow I hadn't.

I closed my eyes and got a terrible feeling in the pit of my stomach. How could I have turned in a paper on a book I hadn't truly read? I had never done that before in my life. I knew what Larry would recommend. He would recommend that I go to my teacher and tell her the truth and accept my punishment and any extra work I might do to make up for my unacceptable behavior.

That's not what I was doing, though. What I was doing was praying with all my might that Ms. Cavelli would find what I wrote more interesting than I knew it actually was.

Ms. Cavelli started walking around the class, handing out papers, and the kids started buzzing when they saw their grades. She has a reputation for being a tough teacher.

"Who'd you write about?" I asked Kimmy, who was sitting at the next desk.

"Richard Wright," she replied. "He was on the list she gave out. I don't think I did very well, though."

At that moment Ms. Cavelli dropped Kimmy's paper on her desk. Face up.

Kimmy's grade was an A. "Well-written!" Ms. Cavelli had scrawled in big red letters across the top of it. "Frame it!"

I smiled. "Congrats. You always get A's, and you always worry."

"So do you," she reminded me, and put the paper in her book bag.

Ms. Cavelli had given out nearly all the papers when she finally gave me mine. She dropped it on my desk. Face down.

Bad sign.

I turned it over, my heart beating a little faster.

B-minus.

"Thin soup," Ms. Cavelli had written. "You can do better than this. Show me on the next one!"

Totally mortified, I quickly stuck the paper under a pile of other papers on my desk.

Kimmy must have seen the look of horror on my face. "You'll do better next time," she said, even though she had no idea what I'd gotten.

Then the bell rang. The whole class emptied out. My next class was lunch, so I was in no hurry, but the other kids had four minutes to get from class to class, which isn't a lot of time, because Green Hills High is a pretty big school. But I just sat there for a moment, contemplating my B-minus.

B-minus. My life was turning into a nightmare. How could this be happening to me?

You have to understand the Farrell family grading system in order to understand why I just sat there. By any objective standard, a B-minus is not an awful grade. It means somewhat better than average.

Not in the Farrell family grading system, created and administered by Lawrence-don't-call-me-Larry Farrell, Howard University valedictorian, class of nineteen-whatever, University of Pennsylvania, Wharton School of Business valedictorian, class of nineteen-whatever. And endorsed through inaction by my mother, who lets Larry run the show when it comes to academics.

"You are smarter than the other kids," I can remember Larry telling me when I was in sixth grade. "You must never fail to work up to your potential at all times."

"Here's where it really starts to count," Larry had told me, the morning of my first day in ninth grade. "No more dress rehearsal. You get a bad grade, you can't turn it around. You want to go to medical school? Well, medical school starts now."

In the Farrell family grading system, B-minus does not mean somewhat better than average. Because average in the Farrell family grading system is A-minus. *A* is what's accepted. A-minus is tolerated. Getting a B means you are close to flunking.

I felt like I'd let everyone down. Including myself.

I got up very slowly and left the room. I could feel Ms. Cavelli's eyes on me, and I felt that she wanted to say something, but she didn't say a word.

Kimmy was waiting for me at the door.

"Was it really that bad?" she asked me softly.

"B-minus," I replied, as we walked toward the cafeteria. "I just can't believe it."

"Maybe Ms. Cavelli will let you do an extra-credit paper or something," Kimmy offered. "Maybe we can write a paper together."

"Maybe what I need to do is concentrate on school," I snapped, irritated.

"Sorry," Kimmy apologized quietly, her tall frame seeming to shrink an inch or two. "I was only trying to help."

"Oh, Kimmy, don't apologize," I said with a sigh. "It's not you. It's me. I'm mad at myself. There just aren't enough hours in the day! I've got to spend more time studying!"

"Well," Kimmy said, "after the Battle of the Bands tomorrow, you should have more time."

"I doubt it," I said with a sigh. "I am seriously overextended."

Kimmy hooked some of her long blond hair behind one ear. "You won't quit the band, though, will you?"

"No," I said, "even though I probably should."

"Oh, no, you shouldn't!" Kimmy protested. "That would be awful!"

I smiled at her. Recently she'd been contemplating quitting the band herself, because she'd gotten so wrapped up in her new boyfriend. We'd all talked her out of that silly notion. "Don't worry, Kimmy, I'm in," I assured her. "I'm just going to have to get up earlier. Or go to bed later. Or something."

At that moment I heard someone calling my name from behind, and I turned around. It was Avery Mandell, my tennis coach, motioning to me from down the hall.

"I'll catch you later," I told Kimmy, and headed over to Avery. "What's up?" I asked him.

"Bad news," Avery said. He's very plainspoken. He told me that he wanted Janine Gilchrist, who played second singles, to play me in a challenge match next week, before our team's big match against John Overton High School.

"But why?" I asked him with alarm.

"She's playing better and better," he said, "and your game is off."

"I'm just in a slump," I protested.

"Maybe," Coach said. "Anyway, I want you to prove to me that you deserve to play number one singles."

"I'll beat her," I told him confidently. I'd played Janine maybe a hundred times since we both started playing competitively. I think she beat me once, two years before, when I was getting over the flu.

"I hope so," Coach Mandell said. "Because you'd look pretty dumb being captain of the team and playing number two singles."

"No problem," I said easily.

Great. Now, on top of everything else, I was going to have to sneak in some extra practice time even if it killed me. The problem was, when?

That afternoon, after tennis practice, I went to The Club at Green Hills, which is located just a few blocks from school on the other side of the Green Hills Mall. I'm a substitute aerobics teacher there—I just fill in now and then when a teacher is out so I can make some pocket money. Another duty I performed there sometimes was orientation for a new member, which was what they'd called me in to do that day. I would show people around and introduce them to the equipment.

I got there five minutes before my orientation and quickly changed from my tennis practice clothes into blue spandex shorts and a Club T-shirt. When I came out of the locker room, I could see a guy sitting in the waiting area. This had to be him.

"Hi," I said, approaching him with my hand out. "I'm Sandra Farrell. I'll be leading your orientation."

He stood up. He was about six feet tall, with a dark, reddish-toned complexion and thick, long, straight black hair. His features were strong, with high cheekbones. He looked to be twenty-two or so.

"Kevin Yellowknife," he said, grinning and reaching his hand out to me.

Native American, I thought. Interesting.

"Glad to meet you," he continued. "Although I wonder if I'll be saying that when we're through!"

I laughed. "It's not so bad," I told him. "Have you been in Nashville long?"

"Three months," was his reply. "Arista Records hired me out of the University of Montana to work in their western music publicity department."

"Sounds interesting," I commented. As cute as he was, my mind was a million miles away. I felt as if I should be studying at that very moment instead of making chitchat at the gym. If I hadn't promised Angela, the gym's manager, that I'd fill in, I'd have been long gone. "So, you ready to get started? Have you ever done this before?"

"No, and do I have to?" he joked.

He was so cute, I had to smile. "Only if you want to be really, really sore tomorrow," I joked back.

"Okay," he said, "let's get to it."

I reached into the fanny pack I was wearing and took out a small bottle of Advil. I shook one out and gave it to him.

"What's that for?" Kevin asked.

"Take it," I instructed. "It's best to take one before your first workout. You'll thank me tomorrow." Obediently, Kevin took the pill.

I walked him down to the gym floor, which was pretty crowded with people training after work. I started to show him the machines and worked with him to create a personal workout routine.

I had just taken Kevin to the seated fly machine—a device that works your chest muscles—and had shown him how to operate it, when I heard a familiar voice from behind me.

"I'm sorry, but I just have to speak up," Jennie Neuman said, trotting over to us. "That's not the way to do it, Sandra!"

Jennie was wearing a pink leotard with pink tights, and she had a large pink ribbon in her hair. She looked like a giant, perky wad of bubble gum.

"Hello, Jennie," I said evenly. "I didn't know you worked out here."

"Well, I just transferred my membership from the Y," she drawled. "I used to work out there all the time." She turned her cornflower-blue eyes on Kevin. "Hello," she simpered.

Kevin looked at me. "You two know each other?"

"From school," I explained, and quickly introduced them.

"Yellowknife," Jennie mused, "that's a unique last name."

"Native American," Kevin explained.

"Really?" Jennie asked, her eyes wide. "That is so interesting!"

"Why?" he asked.

"Well, I never met a genuine Native American before," Jennie explained breathlessly.

Kevin looked puzzled. "What did you do, meet someone who was *pretending* to be a Native American?"

I snorted back my laugh, which Jennie saw. "Oh, I get it. Ya'll are making fun of me."

"Call it good-natured teasing," Kevin insisted cheerfully.

"Oh, it's okay," Jennie assured him. "I can take it. I have a wonderful sense of humor." She turned to me. "Now, Sandra, let me explain something to you. It's much better if you do this exercise with your hands open. You can't cheat that way."

"Jennie," I said in a controlled voice, "why don't you just go work out and let me do my job. Okay?"

"Do your job?" Jennie asked in amazement.

"I work here," I explained patiently.

Jennie sighed. "Well, I'm sorry to interfere, I really am. But I think if you're going to teach people, you should be teaching them correctly!"

"Excuse me," I said to Kevin. "Jennie, can I talk to you a moment? Privately?" I could feel the steel rise in my voice. I took Jennie none too gently by the arm and walked her away from Kevin.

"Listen," I said to her. "I'm just doing my job here, and you just do your workout. Do you get me?"

"Why, Sandra," Jennie said, "you sound upset."

"I'm not upset," I insisted. "I'm just trying to do my work."

"That's good, that you don't get upset easily," Jennie said seriously.

"What are you talking about?" I asked her, keeping my eye on Kevin, who was doing an additional set of reps on the fly machine. He smiled at me; I waved and smiled back.

"I'm talking about how glad I am that you don't get upset easily," Jennie explained. "Because then you won't get all upset over what I'm about to tell you."

"Do you want to just spit it out, Jennie?"

She made a face. "That's such an ugly expression, Sandra. Not very ladylike."

I stared at her. "I know you're not dumb, Jennie," I said slowly. "So for the life of me I cannot figure out why such stupid things come out of your mouth."

"Well, I'm certainly sorry if you don't appreciate the fact that I'm trying to be kind," Jennie sniffed. "The fact of the matter is, some kids at school are about to circulate a recall petition, asking that you be removed as junior class president."

Her words hit me like a fist in my stomach. "I don't believe you," I said.

She shrugged prettily.

"What is it I'm supposed to have done wrong?" I asked her.

"Sandra, you are not the girl we elected," Jennie said gravely. "The class president has to first and foremost be dedicated to the needs of the junior class. Maybe you were at one time, but I think it's pretty clear to everyone that that's not true any longer."

I folded my arms and didn't say a word. Partly because I was afraid I'd kill her and partly because I knew there was some truth to what she was saying.

"I want you to know," Jennie continued, "I've volunteered to take over, should the petition be approved."

"For the good of the school," I said in a low voice.

"Well, of course!" Jennie exclaimed.

"It's your petition, Jennie," I guessed, "yours and Katie Lynn's, I'll bet. And no one is going to impeach me just because you two don't like me."

"Oh, believe me, Sandra," Jennie assured me sweetly, "there's plenty of people who don't like you."

With that she waved to Kevin and sauntered off, the Wicked Witch of the West swathed in pink spandex.

CHAPTER 8

♋

"I'm telling you, Sandra, it was just amazing," Darryl rhapsodized. "I mean, here is this guy who came from nothing, you know? He grew up in the projects, and now he's head of internal medicine at Meharry."

"That's great," I replied, even though I was only half listening.

It was that night, and Darryl and I were sitting in a back booth at Musical Burgers, sipping steaming cups of coffee. I had dressed for our date with extra care, trying to take my mind off our recent fight. I wore a long dress in a purple and lavender floral print, with an antique velvet vest I'd found at a secondhand store, and a velvet choker. Since my usual style was conservative and preppy, I felt kind of daring. Darryl had dressed up, too. He looked unbelievably handsome in pleated black pants, a crisp white shirt, and a full cut black and white houndstooth jacket.

We had just gone to see a production of August Wilson's *The Piano Lesson* at Fisk. At intermission we'd run into Dr. King Phillips, Darryl's personal idol. I'd heard Darryl talk about Dr. Phillips before, but this was the first time I had actually met him. He was a short, balding African American in his late thirties, who exuded a confidence and a charisma that drew people to him. In addition to being head of internal medicine at Meharry, he had started a free clinic where doctors cared for the poor with dignity and respect. Some of the best doctors in Nashville volunteered their services there.

"Did I ever mention that he's named after Martin Luther King?" Darryl asked, his eyes shining.

"Yes, babe, you did," I replied, smiling at Darryl. I loved to see him like this, so enthusiastic and committed. And I loved that we weren't talking about any of the many things that were really on my mind—school, tennis,

Jennie Neuman and her stupid petition, the band, Monroe, lying to my parents. It all just felt so overwhelming.

"I'm going to ask Dr. Phillips if I can volunteer at the clinic," Darryl decided.

"When?" I asked him. "All you have time for now is school, studying, your part-time job, sleeping, and eating."

"And you," Darryl added with a grin. "I have time for you."

"Two Musical Burger specials," the waitress said, delivering our orders and hurrying off.

"Mmm, this looks great," Darryl said, picking up his burger. "I didn't have time to eat dinner."

"Me, either," I agreed, pouring gobs of ketchup onto my burger. I took a big bite. "Mmmm, the best," I mumbled happily, my mouth full.

Darryl took a few huge bites before he spoke again. "Things okay with you and the folks?" he asked me casually.

"Sure," I replied in a guarded voice.

He put his burger down. "They don't know about you seeing Monroe, do they?"

"No," I admitted.

"I got that feeling last night," Darryl said.

"Thank you for not telling them."

Darryl sighed and took a sip of his coffee. "I guess that's your decision, not mine. But you know they only want what's best for you."

"I'm the one who has to decide that," I said stiffly.

"Okay, I concede that," Darryl said. "But in that case you should have the courage of your convictions. Just stand up for your position and tell them the truth. It's not like you to lie."

"I know it isn't," I agreed. I put down my burger. Suddenly I had lost my appetite. "I just . . . I don't want to hurt them," I tried to explain.

"Are you sure?" Darryl asked me. "Or do you just not want to accept responsibility for your own actions?"

That hurt. "No, that's not it," I insisted. "Look, they didn't tell me not to see Monroe, okay? You know how they are—they would never dictate to me. But people don't always say what they really mean."

"Oh, so you're responding to the unspoken message," Darryl said skeptically.

"Yes," I replied. "I am."

Darryl gave me a jaded look and reached for his burger again.

"I *am!*" I repeated.

Darryl kept chewing.

"Look, you can just wipe that I'm-so-superior-and-I-know-better look off your face, okay?"

Darryl gave me a serious look, passed his hand over his face, and came out grinning on the other side. "Better?"

I had to laugh. "Much."

Darryl reached for a french fry and dipped it into some ketchup on my plate. "So, listen, tomorrow night Dr. Phillips is the featured speaker at this symposium on improving health care in disadvantaged populations. You want to go with me?"

"Darryl, you know I can't," I said quietly.

He looked puzzled.

"You know tomorrow night is the Battle of the Bands for Wild Hearts," I reminded him.

He shrugged. "I forgot."

"I don't think so," I said in a low voice. "I think you just pretended to forget."

"I wouldn't do that."

I raised my eyebrows. "Well, then, that means you really forgot, which is worse. You know this is important to me."

"Ya'll want dessert?" the waitress asked, her pencil poised.

"No, thanks," Darryl said.

She laid the check on the table. "I'll just take this whenever you're ready," she said cheerfully, then she refilled our cups before taking off.

Darryl poured some milk into his coffee. "If playing with that band is more important to you than medicine, that's your choice," Darryl said.

I wanted to pound his head in. "That is totally unfair and you know it!"

He sipped his coffee.

Sometimes Darryl fights best by not fighting at all. Savy says he's passive-aggressive—meaning that his passivity is actually very hostile.

I struggled to get control of myself. "Look, I can love music and love playing with the band and still be a good person," I said earnestly. "I can still be serious, I can still want to be a doctor."

"If you say so."

"Darryl, when you get like this I want to kill you," I told him with barely controlled fury.

"It's not me you're mad at, Sandra," he said superciliously.

I rolled my eyes. "Oh, you know better?"

"Your life is out of control," he said simply, as if he had all the answers. "You're mad at yourself."

"No, I'm mad at you," I insisted, throwing my napkin on the table. "I'm sick of your presumed superiority. I'm sick of you knowing better all the time. It's very obnoxious!"

"Hold your voice down," Darryl instructed me in a low, harsh voice. "You don't need to make a scene."

"Maybe I *do* need to make a scene!" I yelled, although probably no one could hear me over the usual late-night din and the country music blasting from the jukebox. "And stop telling me what to do!"

"You are acting like a child," Darryl snapped.

That did it. I grabbed my purse, got up, and ran out of the restaurant.

"I'd offer you some whiskey in that tea, but my mom probably measures the bottle," Jane said, taking a seat on the other side of her kitchen table.

Once I'd hit the street, I'd felt one part fool and one part so angry that I just wanted to get far away from Darryl. But I was too far from my own house to walk home. Then I remembered that the apartment complex where Jane lived was only a couple of blocks away, so I sprinted there. Fortunately she was home—

she'd rented that Oliver Stone movie *The Doors* and had stayed home to watch it. I'd quickly told her that I'd had a fight with Darryl and had run out on my date. She hadn't said a word, just offered me tea and Mystic Mint cookies. And now the whiskey.

"Thanks anyway, I don't drink," I said, taking a sip of the hot tea. "This is good."

She shrugged. "It's Lipton's, and you don't have to be nice." She reached for a cookie and chewed it contemplatively. "So Darryl's being a wanker?"

I sighed. "I don't know. Maybe it's me. I can't believe I just ran out on him."

She grinned. "Hey, I like seeing you do something impetuous for a big change of pace. It means you're human."

"I'm a mixed-up human, is what I am," I said. I rubbed my forehead with my fingers. "God, this just isn't like me! I don't run out of restaurants! My life is in control!"

"Not right now," she observed.

"Well ... well, I don't like this!" I exploded. "It feels awful!"

"Hey, that's how I feel most of the time," Jane said cheerfully. "The way I look at it, being sixteen basically sucks, you know?"

"I want things to be the way they were before."

"Before you met Monroe, you mean?" Jane asked me.

I nodded.

"You mean that?"

"Yes. No. I don't know!" I blurted out. "And it's more than just Monroe. I got another bad grade at school. My tennis coach is all over me, and Jennie Neuman is trying to get me impeached as president of the junior class."

"Oh, God, Jennie Neuman," Jane shuddered. "Well, you can't take her seriously. I mean, she's not very far up on the food chain."

I sighed. "I just feel like I have to start somewhere to get my life back on track. Maybe I should start with Monroe—I don't need him."

"So cut the guy loose," Jane suggested.

"I can't," I admitted. "Okay, I guess I don't really want to." I took a deep breath. "He really opened up to me, you know? But I didn't do the same thing. I just . . . I just presented him with my perfect life, like I had everything all under control. And I don't."

"Yeah, who does?" Jane asked rhetorically.

"I guess I wanted my father to think I did," I admitted.

"Look, he's an incredibly cool person to

CHERIE BENNETT

have as your father," Jane said. "I'd be happy to trade with you, by the way. And I'd appreciate it if you'd take my suck-up little sister, Jilly-poo, in the deal, too."

I fiddled with the tea bag and thought a moment. "I never used to be scared," I finally said in a low voice. "And now I feel scared all the time."

"Join the club," Jane said. She reached for another cookie. "Look, I'm the last person in the world who should give advice to anyone, but . . ."

"But you will," I put in, trying to smile.

"Maybe you should just call Monroe and talk to him. Tell him how you feel. Tell him what's really going on with you."

"You mean tell *him* instead of you," I translated.

"No," Jane said. "I'm flattered, actually, that you came here. I always think of you as being, like, this perfect person."

"Not hardly," I snorted.

"What I mean is," Jane continued, "why don't you tell Monroe the real stuff, too? What, you think he's going to think less of you if you're not superwoman? He doesn't strike me as the kind of guy you have to be perfect for. So why don't you call him?"

110

"You mean . . . now?" I asked, startled.

"Why not?"

I couldn't think of a good reason. "Maybe I should," I said slowly.

She cocked her head toward the wall. "There's the phone," she said and stood up. "I'll go back and watch the end of Jim Morrison—boy, I hate Oliver Stone as a filmmaker, I gotta tell you."

Jane left, and I sat there for several minutes, staring at the phone. Then I finally got up, called Information, and got the number of Monroe's hotel.

"You never had to pretend with me, baby," Monroe said quietly. "Ain't no perfect people in this world."

It was a couple of hours later. When I'd reached Monroe, he'd immediately offered to come pick me up at Jane's in a taxi. Then we'd gone to a jazz club in east Nashville that I'd never been to before. The owner knew Monroe, so they let me in even though I was underage. The first thing I did was to call home so my parents wouldn't worry. I lied and told my mother I was at Jane's house. Then Monroe and I sat in a back booth, the plaintive sounds of a jazz sax drifting over to us from the tiny stage.

I told Monroe about my grades slipping, about Jennie Neuman, about how mad my tennis coach was, and about my fight with Darryl.

"That's a whole lot of pressure," Monroe commiserated. "But I have a feeling you tend to be real hard on yourself, right?"

"I suppose," I agreed. "I mean, I have certain standards . . ."

"Of perfection," Monroe put in.

"Maybe." I twisted my napkin in my fingers nervously. "But Larry says you have to hold yourself to a higher standard if you expect to turn out to be a superior person."

Monroe nodded. "Well, Larry sounds very smart."

"He is," I agreed staunchly.

"I don't have any answers—I guess you know that," Monroe said with a quick grin. "But I do know that life ain't so simple. There's more than one way of looking at things. There's not just one truth for everyone."

I popped one of the ice cubes from my Coke into my mouth. "How do you mean?"

"Well, take school grades, for example. I never did do well in school."

"You dropped out," I pointed out.

"I did," he agreed. "But you know, I don't

regret that decision. Now, maybe you think I should. But school is not for everyone. For an artist, a real artist, I think it can be a waste of time."

"But I have to get A's," I insisted. "I'm number one in the junior class—"

"And I'm proud of you, baby," Monroe said gently. "All I'm saying is that when you get out there in the world, ain't nobody gonna be giving no points for the A's you got in high school."

"But A's will help me get into the best college," I maintained.

"I suppose that's right," Monroe agreed. "I'm just saying that you have to choose your own path, child. It can't be your momma's or Larry's or Darryl's or mine. You see what I'm saying?"

"Maybe," I replied. I jiggled the ice cubes around in my glass and thought a moment. "I never could stand for people to tell me what to do." I looked at him. "Are you like that?"

He nodded. "Just exactly."

"I'm a lot like Larry," I continued. "I mean I'm driven, a perfectionist, which is just like him. But he doesn't mind always following the rules. He loves rules. He says rules are what keeps life from being chaos." I looked at Monroe. "But I'll tell you a secret: sometimes . . . sometimes I just hate rules."

Monroe threw back his head and laughed. "Girl, you got more of me in you than you know."

I sighed. "Darryl loves rules too."

"Your fellow," Monroe said.

"I love him," I explained, "but I feel . . . I feel like sometimes he only loves me if I'm what he wants me to be. Do you know what I mean?"

"You mean like how he doesn't respect your music," Monroe said. "That's a painful thing for you to bear."

"It is!" I agreed. "And he doesn't understand! He says it's not important, that the band is a waste of time—"

"Mm-mm-mm," Monroe murmured under his breath.

"And then when he says that, I start to feel guilty! Like I'm not good enough, I'm not serious enough—"

"That boy is doing a number on you," Monroe said.

"Is he?" I asked faintly.

"Love ain't about judging, and he sure is judging you."

"It makes me feel terrible," I said in a low voice.

"Well, now," Monroe said, "maybe you can understand that that's how your momma made me feel."

I looked into his eyes. "Did she?"

"Don't get me wrong," Monroe said, "she's a wonderful woman. But you can't fit no round peg into no square hole just because someone would like you better square."

I buried my head in my hands. "I don't know what I am. I don't know anything anymore."

Monroe stroked my hair gently. "That's okay, Sandra. You don't have to know. You're doing just fine. You just thought you could figure out all the answers before you even knew the questions. Can't no one do that, baby."

I lifted my face and looked at him. "You won't leave me again, will you?" I whispered. "You'll always be in my life?"

"I'll always be in your life," he promised. "And you will always be the child of my heart."

CHAPTER
9

❦

"You look great, sweetie," my mother told me from the doorway of my bedroom.

It was the next day, Saturday, and I was getting dressed for the Battle of the Bands. We had a few different outfits we wore on stage. We didn't wear matching outfits, which we'd all agreed would be excruciating, but instead we dressed in variations on a theme. Since we had such different tastes and styles, it worked out well.

For the Battle of the Bands we wore our velvet outfits, which we'd found at a second-hand store called Annie's Attic. Since velvet was in style again, anything velvet at the mall or at our favorite shop, Dangerous Threads, was very high-priced. The velvet clothes we'd found at Annie's were from the sixties, things people had given away. I wore ruby-toned velvet jeans with a black and ruby velvet vest. I knew Kimmy would have on her long ruby-red crushed velvet sleeveless dress and hiking boots, Savy would wear the black velvet minidress she'd found, with red cowboy boots, and Jane would have on this great black crocheted minidress over black velvet leggings.

"Thanks, Mom," I replied, slipping into the ballet flats I would wear onstage.

My mom came and sat down on my bed. "You're psyched about this, huh?"

I smiled at her reflection in the mirror as I put on some light lipstick. My mom still sounds exactly how she probably sounded when she was a twenty-year-old hippie. You can imagine how funny her conversations sometimes sound with the exceedingly proper Lawrence-don't-call-me-Larry.

"So you guys have a shot at winning?" my mom asked idly.

"No," I replied honestly. "I mean, we're good. We're really good. But we haven't been together long enough to win."

"Oh, well, that's not what's important," my

mom said breezily. "It's the music, you know?"

I sat down next to her on my bed. "Is that really how you feel?"

She shrugged. "People get so competitive with this music thing—it hasn't changed any since I was coming up. People can get really ugly about it, you know? It's a bummer."

"I do know," I agreed. "But . . . didn't you ever want to just fight to become a star? I mean, don't you ever get depressed, just singing behind other artists?"

"No," my mother replied honestly. "I really don't."

"But don't you think that if you're truly gifted you should do more with that gift?" I pressed.

She laughed. "Oh, does that mean you think you mother is truly gifted?"

"You know I do," I replied seriously.

She brushed some lint off my bedspread. "I don't think I probably have the temperament for that," she said thoughtfully.

"Or maybe you were afraid of failure," I suggested.

She looked surprised. "No, I don't think so. Being a star just never meant enough to me."

"Well, that's you," I said. "But can you understand how someone else with incredible talent and passion couldn't possibly settle for being a backup anything? Or for not playing his or her own music?"

She looked at me closely. "Who are we talking about here?"

"It's hypothetical," I replied, not meeting her gaze.

"Well, then, hypothetically I can understand that," my mother said slowly. "But I have a feeling we're talking about more than a hypothesis here, babe. Have you been—"

"Ah, my two beauties," Larry said, appearing in the doorway with a steaming cup of tea. He took a sip. "You arrived home late last night," he observed.

"I decided not to stay over at Jane's after all," I replied. I jumped up and busied myself putting on a choker necklace and some tiny cross earrings.

"I see," Larry said. "Did you have a nice time?"

"It was okay," I said guardedly.

He sipped his tea again. "And what made you decide to leave Jane's in the middle of the night to come home?"

"Look, I don't have to report to you," I snapped guiltily.

Larry looked hurt, and I felt like an idiot. "I didn't mean to imply that you did, Sandra," he replied with dignity.

My mother was staring at me knowingly, and I was getting very nervous about the turn this conversation was taking.

"Wish me luck," I told them both, slinging the strap of my purse over my shoulder. I picked up my bass case, kissed them both, hoping my kiss would suffice as a sort of apology to Larry, then headed for the front door.

"Kimmy, you look green," Jane said.

We were all backstage in one of the dressing rooms at the Performance Space, where the big Teen Battle of the Bands was taking place. Each local contest was sponsored by a college or university, and ours was being sponsored by Vanderbilt. There were thousands of contests taking place all over the country. The only rule was that at least half of the members of each band had to be teens, and all had to be full-time high school or college students. The local winners would compete statewide, and the statewide winners would then compete nationally.

From the intercom speaker in the corner, we could hear what was going on onstage. A group called Rubber Band was on. They combined New Wave—which was now old wave—with rap. I thought they were awful. We would go on tenth, which meant we still had quite a wait.

I peered at Kimmy. She really did look awful. "You want some water or something?" I asked her. "Some Coke?"

"Coke?" she asked, turning greener. "Oh, no, I think I'm going to—" She ran into the nearby ladies' room.

"Oh, just great," Jane said, nervously bouncing her drumsticks off the coffee table.

"I'll go see if she's okay," Savy offered, hurrying after Kimmy.

"Don't worry about it," I told Jane. "You know Kimmy almost always gets sick before we go on."

"That's true," Jane said. "I just keep thinking it's a temporary thing, and she'll get over it."

"She's always okay by the time we go on," I reminded Jane.

"Well, with Kimmy I never feel totally confident," Jane replied. She drummed a fast riff on the table. "So, how'd it go last night?"

"Really . . . really well," I told her. "I want to thank you for suggesting I call Monroe."

Jane shrugged. "That's what buds are for," she said airily. She pulled at the crotch of her stretch velvet leggings. "Did they cut things smaller in the sixties or something? This is cutting off my circulation."

I didn't reply, I just looked at my watch for maybe the twentieth time since we'd arrived. "I think my watch stopped. What time is it?"

"Two minutes later than it was the last time you asked me," Jane said. "Monroe will get here."

"This is dressing room C, right?" I asked. I opened the door to check the letter on it. "I was so sure I told him dressing room C." I left the door open and peered out into the hall.

"He'll get here," Jane said like a broken record.

"But what if he doesn't?" I asked.

"Sandra, if he doesn't get here you will go out there and do the same incredible job you would have done if he'd been here," Jane stated.

"Yes, of course," I said. "But ... he said he'd be here."

"See, this is a perfect example of why a person is better off having a polite but distant relationship with her parental units," Jane said.

"You don't see me waiting for my dad to mosey into the dressing room. My parents have this sort of distant but pleasant attitude toward the band, which is just the way I like it."

I peered out into the hallway again. "It's too bad Savy's family isn't here," I said, even though of course it wasn't Savy's family I was looking for. "You think she's upset about it?"

Jane shook her head no. "She's more upset about Gramma Beth having another fainting spell, would be my guess," Jane observed. "You know if it wasn't for that, they'd all be here, overflowing with all that Leeman family enthusiasm." Jane knocked her drumsticks in a staccato beat against her boots. "Ever notice how cute Savy's older brothers are?" she added idly.

I laughed. "No, I've been living under a rock and hadn't noticed."

Jane shrugged. "Well, you're always so cool about things like that." She wiggled her eyebrows at me. "I mean, have you ever been just, like, carried away by lust in your entire life?"

"No," I replied truthfully. "I would never let that happen."

"I don't mean carried away to the point of doing something you're going to regret deeply in the morning," Jane qualified. "I mean like when you see a guy and you just say to yourself, 'I have to have him.' "

"No," I said, pacing the room nervously. "How would I know if I had to have him, based on just his appearance? As far as I'm concerned, attraction goes much deeper than that."

"God, if I was as mature as you are, my parents would think they had died and gone to heaven," Jane muttered.

"Everything's fine," Savy assured us as she ushered Kimmy back into the dressing room.

Kimmy sat down on the couch next to Jane. She looked white now instead of green.

"I'm really sorry, ya'll," Kimmy said. "I just get so nervous. I wish I didn't!"

"It's better than hurling onstage," Jane said philosophically.

Kimmy's eyes got huge. "Can you imagine? Oh, God, what if that happens? What if I actually get sick onstage?"

"That won't happen, child," a deep voice said from the doorway.

Monroe.

"Once you're out there, you'll be a queen," he told her magnificently.

Kimmy smiled and seemed to believe him.

"I'm so glad you're here," I told him, hurrying over to give him a big hug.

"I wouldn't have missed this for the world," he told me, kissing my forehead.

"You were so late," I said. "I thought maybe—"

"I had a phone call from France," he explained. "It took some time."

Something in his eyes caught my attention, something bad.

"Are you okay?"

"Sure," he said with a grin. But his eyes didn't grin. I noticed tiny dots of sweat on his forehead. And it wasn't warm in the dressing room.

"Mr. LaCrue, you're gonna be our good-luck charm," Jane decreed. "I can feel it."

"We're going to be fabulous!" Savy cried. "We are!"

"Look, we can't possibly win," I pointed out pragmatically.

"Negative thinking!" Savy chided me.

"No, it's realism. Maybe two years from now, but not yet," I said.

"I just don't believe that," Savy maintained.

Through the speaker we heard applause.

"Give it up for Rubber Band!" the MC, a deejay from a local rock station was saying.

As he said a few words, I knew the stage was revolving so that the next band—whose equipment had been set up on the revolving stage during the previous act—could rotate into place.

"And now, ladies and gentlemen, from University of Tennessee, please welcome four fine ladies with killer voices, Dangerous Curves!"

"Oh, please, gag me in a major way," Jane snorted. "A girl group who calls itself Dangerous Curves?"

"Hello, Nashville!" the lead singer of Dangerous Curves was yelling into the microphone. "Put your hands together!"

A funky backbeat started, and I could hear people in the audience clapping in rhythm. The band kicked in. They sounded good. I got more nervous. Kimmy turned green again.

"Hey, same old same-old!" Monroe said encouragingly. "They don't sound fresh. Now, *you* ladies sound fresh!"

"Are you sure?" Kimmy asked in a quavery voice.

"Sweetheart, I know music," Monroe said simply, "and I'm telling you God's truth." He held up his hand solemnly.

"Thanks," I whispered, giving him another hug.

"Knock 'em dead, you hear me?" he whispered back. "Well, ladies, I will go out into the audience. The fool you hear screaming and shouting when you hit the stage will be me."

"I'll walk you out there," I offered.

As we strolled down the hallway, I looked at Monroe out of the corner of my eye. He had that troubled look on his face again.

"Hey, are you sure nothing is wrong?" I asked him.

"Baby, everything is copacetic," he insisted.

"Copacetic?" I repeated, puzzled.

He laughed. "I guess you don't hear that expression too much anymore. It means way cool," he explained floating his hand through the air in a horizontal line to illustrate his point.

"Is that child always so nervous before she goes onstage?" Monroe asked me lightly, obviously referring to Kimmy.

"Yes, to tell you the truth," I replied. "Usually I don't know whether to shake her or feel sorry for her, but to tell you the truth, tonight I'm almost as nervous as she is."

Monroe smiled. "I'll tell you a secret. I used to get real nervous before I went on. I remember the most scared I ever was. I was in Paris, and I got a phone call asking me could I sit in with Miles Davis, because his keyboard player was ill. Miles was one of my all-time idols. I was so nervous backstage I thought I would up and die. And Miles, he sees me looking all green and shaking like a drunk before payday, and he says to me, 'Monroe, what you need is a goodluck charm.' And then he gave me this."

Out of his pocket Monroe pulled a red heart-shaped charm attached to a key chain. The name Miles Davis was scrawled in gold script across the heart.

"You still have it," I murmured.

"And for tonight, *you* have it," Monroe said, putting the heart into my hand and closing my fingers around it. "It's worked magic for me every time, and it can work the same magic for you."

"Thanks," I said, and held the heart tightly in my hand.

We stopped just before we got to the stage exit. I noticed that strange look in Monroe's eyes again. Something sad, weary—scared, even.

"I just want you to know that you can talk to me," I told him in a low, intense voice. "I mean *really* talk to me. "It's a two-way street, right?"

His eyes clouded over again. I knew he was going to say something—something important—but at that exact moment the stage door opened and there stood three familiar people.

My mom, Larry, and Darryl.

The five of us just stood there, staring at each other. Darryl regained the power of speech first.

"We came to surprise you," he said, staring at Monroe.

"Well, I'm surprised all right," I agreed in a flat voice. I took a deep breath. And I introduced everyone to everyone. What else could I do?

Larry stuck his hand out first. Monroe shook it. Then Monroe shook hands with Darryl. As for my mother, she just stared at Monroe.

"What are you doing here?" she finally said.

"My daughter invited me," Monroe replied.

She looked at me. "You've been seeing each other, I take it."

"Yes," I admitted defiantly.

"In other words, you've been lying to us," my mother continued in a cold voice.

"Yes," I said.

"It's not the child's fault—" Monroe began.

"She is not a child," my mother said. "And she is certainly responsible for her actions. And for telling the truth."

"Look, I'm sorry," I began, then I stopped. "No. No, I'm not sorry. I'm sorry I lied to you, but I'm not sorry I've been seeing my father."

I saw the look on Larry's face when I called Monroe my father, and I would gladly have done five years' hard time to take back my thoughtless comment. But there. It was said.

And there was nothing I could do to take it back.

"Please welcome a band that's hot as well as original," the MC said. "Put your hands together for Wild Hearts!"

As the turntable stage that we were all standing on rotated, I quickly felt the outline of the heart-shaped key charm that I'd stuck into my pocket. I locked eyes with Savy and she gave me a dazzling grin, and then we were in front of all those people—hundred of eyes staring at us, waiting.

"Oh, God," Kimmy squeaked as we stared out at the sea of faces.

Everything is fine, I chanted in my own

mind. Don't think about what just happened. Concentrate on the music.

But in a flash all those faces swam before my eyes—Monroe, Darryl, Larry, and Mom—and I remembered every awful moment that I'd lived through before we went onstage.

I had never ever thought that my parents and Darryl would come to see the Battle of the Bands. Larry hated country and rock music—he listened to opera. Darryl tolerated it (though he preferred jazz), mostly because he knew I liked a lot of it. And my mother was immersed in it all day long. None of them had a really good reason to come to hear Wild Hearts, except that they loved me and they wanted to surprise me. And there I was, sneaking around with Monroe. I was a traitor. And a liar. And I had just made one of the biggest verbal gaffes of my life.

It was like my worst nightmare come true.

Savy had rescued me. She'd come out to check on me, to bring me back into our dressing room so we could have a few quiet moments together before we went onstage. So she'd seen me out there twisting in the wind.

"Hi!" she'd said, as if our gathering was something that happened every day.

"Listen," she had continued nonchalantly, "the band's got some stuff to go over, so I'm just gonna have to pull Sandra away from ya'll. Okay?"

What could they do but nod yes? And that's exactly what they did.

"We'll see ya'll afterward," Savy said, by way of saying good-bye. Then she took me by the arm and led me back to our dressing room.

"Woah, baby, Sandra," she began to say, "I can't believe—"

"Forget it," I cut her off quickly.

"But—"

"Forget it," I insisted as we went back inside. "It's no biggie."

"What's no biggie?" Jane asked, looking up from a magazine she'd been pretending to read.

I couldn't pull it off. I buried my face in my hands in misery. And humiliation. And then I told them all what had just happened.

As I talked, I watched Kimmy's complexion, which had been edging toward green again, slowly make its way back through the color spectrum toward a healthy pink.

Nothing like someone else's problems to get your mind off your own.

Everyone in the band started saying nice things to me, trying to tell me that it wasn't so bad, that after we went on, I'd have a chance to get everything straightened out. I tried to believe them, but it was hard.

Still, I knew what was really important—the band. And I knew that's what was important to them, too. I had to go out there and give the best performance of my life. Not for Monroe, not for my parents or for Darryl. For myself.

"Hello out there," Savy called into her vocal mike, jolting me back to reality. "We're Wild Hearts, and don't you forget it!" Then she counted us in, and we launched into what was rapidly becoming our signature tune, our rocked-out four-part-harmony version of "It Wasn't God Who Made Honky Tonk Angels." I think it's because we were all a little nervous that we took it even faster than normal, with Jane's feet on the bass drum and high hat powering us along. But it sounded even better, I thought—more rock than country.

The crowd loved it. We'd heard some pretty traditional country bands backstage through the tinny speaker in our dressing room, and in my humble opinion none of them had sounded half as good as we did.

The applause was prolonged and enthusiastic, washing over us like love. I grinned at Kimmy, who looked light-years away from the scared green waif who'd been upchucking backstage. She threw her blond hair insouciantly back behind her shoulders and played the opening riff to Jane's original, "Runnin' Scared." Savy came in on the verse, and we all joined in on the chorus. I gave it my all, running my bass licks with my eyes closed, lost in the music. When we finished, the audience again burst into applause, appreciative and sustained. It wasn't like the wild reaction to our opening number—everyone knew that tune, and our arrangement was very hot—but it was still great. We did another original of Jane's, "Love's Gone Away," and then finished with a hard-rocking blowout version of "Great Balls of Fire" by Jerry Lee Lewis: "Goodness, gracious, great balls of fire!"

We jammed out the last sustained chords, Savy jumped in the air, and we came to a burning, crashing finish. The crowd cheered and roared their approval, whistling and stomping their feet. I felt like I was flying! Normally when I'm onstage I can't see the audience because the bright stage lights are blinding. But a follow spot was trained on the audience, making circles, illuminating various faces in the crowd. For just an instant I saw Larry, who was standing about fifteen rows deep in the audience. His mouth was open in shock—I hoped good shock, I couldn't tell for sure—and standing next to him was Darryl, who had his arms folded defensively but had a slight smile on his face, as if he couldn't decide what emotion to feel.

"Thank you very much!" Savy yelled into her mike over the cheering crowd. "We're Wild Hearts," and then all of us yelled together into our mikes, "and don't you forget it!" Then we ran offstage.

As usual we hugged each other with the sheer exuberance we usually felt when we came offstage. We had been good. Really, really good. Maybe even great.

"Awesome!" Savy shrieked. "I know we won!"

"We did kick butt," Jane agreed happily.

"Wow!" Kimmy cried happily. "That was actually fun!"

Yeah. Fun. But as I came down from my high, all I could think was that it was definitely *not* going to be any fun when I faced up to my mom and Larry and Darryl.

But that was later. First there was the rest

of the contest, and then the announcement of the winners. Maybe, just maybe, we really did have a chance of winning.

With that thought, I felt more confident. I could handle anything, even my family. I was Monroe LaCrue's daughter, and he had heard us and seen us perform in all our glory. I was an adult. I made my own decisions. And that was what I was going to tell them all.

So why did I feel like I was going to my own funeral?

CHAPTER
10

$\heartsuit$

Do you think we really have a chance?" Kimmy asked me anxiously as we joined all the other bands whose members were assembling in a huge special holding area backstage.

"Sssh!" Jane shushed her. "They're starting!" She pointed to the MC, who had taken his place by the microphone at center stage.

We all grabbed each other's hands nervously, clutching on for dear life. I was completely caught up in the suspense. I had gone from the ease of thinking we didn't have a prayer to the white-knuckle anxiety of thinking we did.

"Look, we shouldn't get our hopes up," I

told the others. "Remember, we've only been together a few weeks."

"So?" Savy asked.

"So I saw Heaven's Gate, that Christian rock band from Belmont College, a year ago," I explained. "They were the opening act for Michael Smith. And they were already great then."

Jane eyed the girls from Dangerous Curves, who were standing together off to our right. They were all dressed in skimpy skintight spandex and leather, wearing so much makeup that it pretty much obscured their faces. "As long as we don't lose to them," Jane said. "They are everything I hate about girl bands."

"They sounded good, though," Kimmy pointed out.

"They were okay," Jane said grudgingly. "But I mean look at them! They're selling sleaze and sex, not music."

"So, guy musicians do that all the time," Savy said. She clutched my hand tighter. "Please let us win," she chanted, her eyes closed.

"Okay, all you music lovers!" the MC yelled into the microphone. "It's time to announce the winners of the Nashville Teen Battle of the Bands. Here's how it works. We award prizes to the top five bands. The first and second place bands will go to the Tennessee State Teen Battle of the Bands, which will be held out at Opryland. As I announce each prize, I'd like the winning band to come up on stage. Now, before I announce the winners, how about a round of applause for all sixteen bands who played for us tonight?"

The crowd dutifully applauded.

"In fifth place, winner of one hundred dollars, four gorgeous ladies, Dangerous Curves!" the MC cried.

The four girls in Dangerous Curves screamed and ran out from the holding area onto the stage. The crowd whooped and whistled. My heart sank. When the MC had said "four gorgeous ladies," I had felt sure that he was talking about us.

"Okay, if we don't place higher than them I'm going to kill myself," Jane stated.

"I doubt that we will," I replied. "They'll never pick two all-girl groups."

"That's not true," Savy maintained staunchly. "They don't pick on the basis of sex."

"Sha, right," Jane snorted. And as if to prove her point, fourth prize was awarded to one of the traditional country groups we'd heard while we were in our dressing room, a band named Rocky Road.

"Yum-yum," Jane joked, "I can just taste that Musical Burgers special right about now. Because there's no reason for us to stay."

"Wait," Savy said, though I could see she was just trying to put up a good front.

As for Kimmy, her shoulders had sagged noticeably. "Now I'm glad Sawyer had to go to Memphis with his parents," she sighed. "I'd be so embarrassed if he saw us get shut out."

"Third place!" the MC cried, getting our attention again, "the winner of four hundred dollars in cash, goes to a very hot original new band that I believe has a huge future . . . Wild Hearts—and don't you forget it!"

We all looked at each other a second, and then we screamed.

"That's us!" Savy screamed. "Oh, my God! We did it!" We won, we won!" Savy jumped up and down. She threw her arms around me, which would have been really nice, but I was already hugging Jane.

I don't know how it happened—I assure you it was not planned—but the four of us somehow joined hands as we ran out onstage. The MC told us to take a bow, and we did just that. It didn't even matter that Kimmy's bow was more like sort of a ducking of her head. Then the MC handed Savy an envelope containing four hundred dollars in cash, which Savy promptly handed to me. I held it up over my head in a gesture of triumph.

We ran offstage laughing and babbling excitedly. The MC announced the second- and first-place winners, but we were so high we didn't pay a lot of attention. In second place was a heavy metal band called Jump! and then Heaven's Gate, the Christian rock band I'd heard the year before, took the grand prize.

"If only we'd placed second, we'd get to play in the state finals," Jane said, as the MC finished talking into the mike.

"Hey, we did great!" Savy cried happily. "We did amazing!"

And then the strangest thing happened. Just as the MC was asking the five winning bands to join him onstage, a skinny guy from the Hulk, a heavy metal band that hadn't placed, walked out onstage and actually took the mike from the MC.

"I'm Rex Baker from the Hulk," he said into the mike, "and I want to lodge a protest."

A murmur spread through the crowd, then the house grew quiet with expectation. The MC looked too taken aback to respond.

"I have to tell you that all the guys in Jump! except their new drummer are over twenty," Rex said into the mike. "Their lead guitar player is twenty-four years old, man. I mean, fair is fair, and this ain't fair."

The MC grabbed the mike back. "We'll have to settle this later," he said. "Now, if the winning bands would—"

"Hey, it's true!" one of the other guys from the Hulk yelled from behind me. "Check their driver's licenses!"

"Yeah, check!" someone in the audience yelled out.

"Check! Check! Check!" the crowd began to chant, the roar growing stronger.

"Okay," the MC finally said. "You gotta give the public what they want!"

"Hey, this is bogus, man!" the lead guitarist from Jump! cried, storming onto the stage.

"Fair is fair," the MC said cheerfully. "Besides, I don't want to get stoned by this crowd. Could the guys from Jump! all come out here and turn over your driver's licenses?"

Reluctantly the band straggled out onto the stage.

The lead guitarist handed over his license, then the others did, too. The MC scanned them quickly, then reached for the mike.

"Sorry, you guys are great musicians, but you're disqualified on account of age."

"We got rooked, man," the drummer yelled. The band left the stage in disgust.

The crowd grew quiet, waiting to see what would happen. Quickly the MC conferred with the head judge, an artists-and-repertory guy from Liberty Records. Then he came back to the microphone. "Because Jump! has been disqualified, we'll have a new fifth-place band—the judges are figuring that out now. And the bands in fifth, fourth, and third place will all move up one place."

Savy grabbed my hand so hard she practically broke the bones in my fingers. "Do you realize what this means? We're second place!"

"We're in the state finals!!" Jane screamed.

Kimmy and I screamed, too. We all jumped up and down, screaming, crying, carrying on. It was one of the most exciting moments of my life. We didn't even hear who the new fifth-place band was when the announcement was made. I was *that* happy. Not just for myself but also for the band. And, I'll admit it, because I'd had something to prove, and I had proved it.

To everybody.

* * *

We went out onto the stage for the winners' photo, and the MC took back our envelope with the four hundred dollars for third place and handed us another envelope containing the six hundred dollars we'd just won for second place. Then we ran back to dressing room C, screaming and laughing with joy. I was still floating on air when I went out to look for my parents and for Darryl. Savy offered to come with me—she is just so thoughtful sometimes—but I told her no, I needed to do this by myself.

There was only one problem.

When I went out into the area near the stage door, they weren't there. And they weren't in the audience section, either. Or in the lobby.

They were all gone. And I was irritated. Regardless of my mistake in judgment, they should have stayed afterward to congratulate me, and to give me the opportunity to make things right.

When I got back to the dressing room, they weren't there waiting for me, either. Monroe was, though, and he threw his arms around me and lifted me into the air.

"You did it, child," he said to me warmly. "You went and did it."

"Thanks," I said to him, and I meant it.

"You girls can go as far as you want to go, you know that," he said seriously.

"What do you know?" Jane teased. "Country music is not exactly your thing. Of course, it's not mine, either."

"Well, for a girl who ain't into country, you sure can play it," Monroe replied, his eyes shining. "Besides, good music is good music. And you ladies are *good.*"

"I can't believe we just won six hundred big ones," Jane marveled. "Hey, I've got a great idea."

"What?" Kimmy asked, coiling her hair on top of her head and fanning the back of her neck.

"Let's vote to give me all the money right this second," Jane suggested, taking a big swig of soda from a can she was holding. "I'll apply it to my debt to my parents and I can quit slaving away at Uncle Zap's."

"Great idea!" Savy said, egging Jane on.

"No way," I said firmly, fanning the air with the envelope full of money. "This is for the band. We've got music to copy, demos to make . . . six hundred dollars won't even begin to cover our expenses."

"Hey, we should open a Wild Hearts bank account!" Savy suggested.

We all agreed, and I volunteered to go to the bank with the money the next day.

"This is only the beginning for you ladies," Monroe said warmly. "You will have major success, and you deserve it."

I smiled at him gratefully. Monroe. At least *he* was sticking by me. My boyfriend and my parents had just run out, like it didn't even matter to them how well I'd done. Oh, I knew in my heart how badly I had hurt them. I would have been the first one to admit that Larry had a really good reason to be upset with me, and my mother had a good reason too. Darryl I'm not so sure about. He was acting more like one of my parents than like my boyfriend. But couldn't they have just let it go for a few minutes and have come backstage to congratulate the band and me?

I felt like all the hard work I did, all my accomplishments, were wiped out in their eyes by one stupid mistake. How fair was that?

There was a knock at the door. My heart leaped. Maybe it was my parents and Darryl. But it was only one of the organizers of the contest, telling us that we had to come out for another photo. The other girls started to leave, but I wanted just a couple of minutes alone with Monroe, so I could tell him how I felt.

"I'll catch up with you," I told them.

"Don't miss it," Kimmy said, her face suffused with happiness. "We're not a band without you."

I grinned and waved them on.

"Great group," Monroe said to me quietly.

"I know," I said. "Listen, I just wanted to thank you for coming here tonight and coming backstage and rooting for us."

Monroe smiled a gentle smile. "That's what love is, child," he said to me. "That's just what love is." A dark cloud seemed to pass over his face.

"What?" I asked him anxiously.

"I just want you to know that I'm sorry, Sandra," he said quietly. "All those years I lost with you . . ."

"It's okay," I said quietly.

"No, it really isn't," he insisted. "But what's done is done." I saw his eyes flick over the envelope of cash that bulged from my pocket, then he looked me straight in the eye. "I'm not a perfect person, baby. I wish I were."

"You're wonderful," I insisted. Something in the room felt strange, some terrible tension I couldn't name. "Hey, your lucky charm worked!" I cried, trying to lighten the mood. I pulled the heart key chain from my pocket.

"You keep it," Monroe said.

"No," I said emphatically, practically pushing it at him. "I want you to hold it hostage, so that you can bring it to our next show."

Monroe smiled. "Okay, *ma jolie fille*," he said quietly, calling me "my beautiful daughter" in French. "I'll hold it hostage. Now, you'd better get out there for your moment of glory."

"You're right," I said. As I got ready to go, I put the envelope containing the cash we'd won in my pocketbook and stuck the pocketbook under a chair.

"You'll be here when I get back?" I asked him.

He just smiled at me, but I knew what that meant. I threw my arms around him and hugged him hard, then I ran out to the stage to join my friends.

And I tried to ignore the nagging, scary feeling that something was terribly, terribly wrong with Monroe, something he wasn't telling me.

But maybe it was just my imagination. Yes, that's what it had to be.

The photo session took forever, and then there were questions from some guy from a newspaper, and from a couple of reporters from school papers as well.

By the time I finally got back to the dressing room, Monroe was gone. Well, I couldn't blame him, really. I figured I'd just call him at the hotel the next day. No big thing. We packed up all our stuff and decided to skip Musical Burgers for a change and go to the more upscale Green Hills Grille to talk and continue our celebration.

We deserved it.

"Kimmy," Jane said, swallowing a bite of the Green Hills Grille's Vegetarian Garden Burger, "I gotta tell ya, I thought you were gonna hurl right there onstage."

Kimmy blushed. "Did I look that awful?"

"Worse!" Savy exclaimed happily, taking a giant gulp of iced tea. "I had a spare paper bag under my microphone just in case."

"Okay, okay," Kimmy said. "I was nervous. Weren't you?"

She looked around the table at all of us. We all shook our heads, somber expressions on our faces.

Then Savy cracked up. "Of course I was nervous, you bozo! But we were so hot!"

"We were good," I said matter-of-factly, "but we still have a lot of work to do. There are ten thousand people in Nashville who are good."

"If you'd give me that money we won," Jane repeated, "we could do that work a lot faster. I wouldn't have to work at that idiot job. I feel like zombie-woman there."

"At least you get to buy CDs cheap," Savy pointed out.

"Yeah, but with what chip?" Jane asked, using a New York City slang expression for "money." "Everything I earn I'm handing right over to the parental units to pay for that scum-bucket Wyatt Shane wrecking my mom's car."

"Well, look at it this way," Savy said. "If Wyatt hadn't broken his arm while driving drunk, his band would have been up there tonight. So in a way you got some revenge."

"Nah," Jane said, dipping a corn chip into the spinach-artichoke dip. "Because we would have wiped Thunder Rolls off the stage, which would have been very, very satisfying." She reached for another corn chip. "Boy, going out with him was one of the stupider moments of my life."

"You won't get any argument from us," I told her, reaching for a french fry.

"Oh, yeah, Miss Cool," Jane teased. "So what if you and Darryl are practically married? Some of us are still young enough to crave a little adventure!"

"Wyatt isn't adventure," Kimmy said darkly. She sighed. "I miss Sawyer."

"You were just with him yesterday," Savy reminded her.

"So?" Kimmy said. "I want to be with him all the time."

"Why don't you just have yourself joined to him at the hip?" Jane suggested sarcastically.

"Oh, I can think of better places to be joined," Kimmy replied with studied innocence.

We all hooted with laughter.

"Why, Kimmy, you sly dog," I teased her. "Still waters run deep, huh?"

Savy gave Kimmy a look. "Just how far have you and Sawyer gone?"

"Not very," Kimmy replied, blushing.

"How far is 'not very'?" Jane asked. "I have to hear the gory details, since as far as guys are concerned I lead an empty and meaningless life."

"Can we change the subject?" Kimmy asked. "I'm still as pure as the driven snow, if that's what you're wondering."

"So sweet, so young, so virginal!" Jane sang out.

Kimmy made a face. "It happens to be true. The only one who doesn't believe it is my mother, who thinks I'm a slut." She sighed. "I don't want to talk about her. I want to talk about the band, okay?"

"Okay," Savy agreed. "But I just want to say that if your mother thinks bad things about you, it's her problem, because we know how totally cool you are."

"I'll second that," I added.

Kimmy looked at me gratefully.

"Okay, Wild Hearts," Savy said, "we've had our first huge success. What's next for us?"

"We're going to Disneyland!" Jane cried, in imitation of the TV commercials.

We all cracked up.

"But seriously, folks—" Savy began.

"The state finals!" Kimmy cried happily.

"Music videos on MTV!" Jane added.

"I think we're more CMT," Savy replied, referring to Country Music Television, the twenty-four-hour country-music video channel on cable.

"Let's not get carried away," I said. "I think we need to practice more before we start talking about videos." I picked somewhat daintily at a pile of french fries on my plate. I was quickly losing my appetite, because I had just looked at my watch, and I'd seen how late it was. Much as I'd have loved to just hang with the band forever, I knew I would have to go home and face the music with my parents.

In fact, the time was now.

I stood up.

"What are you doing?" Savy asked.

I told them, then I reached for my purse to pay for my food.

"Hey, it's on my parents," Savy said, stopping me. "They gave me bucks to pay for us to go out tonight, and said to tell us how sorry they were they couldn't be there."

"I wish I had parents like that," Kimmy said quietly.

"Thank them for me," I told Savy. I slung the strap of my purse over my shoulder. "Tomorrow the six hundred dollars in here starts our official Wild Hearts bank account," I added with satisfaction.

"Hey, good luck with the 'rents," Jane said. "I know how bizarro they can be. Just remember, no matter what happens, we're with you, Sandra."

"Right," Savy agreed.

"Right," Kimmy echoed firmly. "We're in this together."

It was Kimmy who first hesitantly reached her hand across the table to the middle. Jane then did the same thing, taking Kimmy's hand. Then Savy did the same thing.

Then I felt my hand being pulled like a magnet to join theirs.

I wasn't alone.

CHAPTER
11

♡

*T*hey were waiting up for me.

Somehow I had known they would be.

I found Larry and my mom sitting in the living room, drinking wine together for the second time in a week.

I sat on the couch opposite them. "We came in second," I told them. "We won six hundred dollars and we're going to the state finals."

"Congratulations," my mother said coolly.

"You could have stayed to see if we won," I said. "That would have been nice."

"A lot of things would have been nice, Sandra," my mother said. "Like your telling us the truth, for example."

I looked at Larry. He sipped at his wine, a hurt look on his face.

"I'm sorry I lied," I told them. "I already apologized, if you recall."

"We recall," my mother said. "But why is it that I'm still so angry?"

"I don't know." I sighed. "You tell me."

She looked over at Larry, as if asking him to take the ball and run with it.

"I suppose we feel betrayed in a certain way," Larry began slowly.

I felt horrible when he said that. "Look, I'm not perfect—"

"And neither are we," Larry broke in gently. "But we do tell you the truth. Scrupulously. And we expect the same from you."

"I didn't want to hurt you," I mumbled.

"And yet you have," Larry said. "Much more so than if you had just told us your decision was to see your father in the first place."

I gulped hard. I wanted to protest, to say what I always said to Larry: "He's not my father. You're my father." But everything felt so mixed up, nothing was clear, so I didn't say anything about that at all. "When did Darryl leave?" I asked them.

"He left with us," my mother said.

"Why doesn't he just date the two of you?" I said irritably. "Sometimes I think he cares about you more than he cares about me."

"He was being considerate," Larry said formally.

"Which is more than I can say for you," my mother added.

"Okay, I was inconsiderate!" I cried, jumping up from the couch. "I'm sorry! I'm really, really sorry! What is it that you want me to do?"

"You could begin by sitting down, calming down, and not making a scene," Larry suggested.

"I *feel* like making a scene!" I yelled. "God, between you and Darryl I feel strangled by propriety! I'm upset, okay?"

"Oh, just chill out, Sandra," my mother groused. "We have feelings, you know. We're hurt. You hurt us by lying to us. Now you're ticked off because we have the audacity to have feelings you don't want us to have."

"That goes both ways," I hurled back at her.

"We are not the ones who broke a family trust," my mother pointed out.

I sat back down. "Couldn't you just punish me?" I asked them in a low voice. "Couldn't we just get it over with?"

Larry sipped his wine again. "I suppose the problem, Sandra, is that we can't think of anything appropriate to do. This isn't like breaking curfew. This has more to do with your personal code of ethics."

"It doesn't," I insisted. "I mean that I do have ethics—the ones you've taught me. I just . . . I made a stupid decision." I looked down at the carpet and felt miserable.

Larry leaned forward and touched my hand. "We know you have ethics, Sandra. But . . . sometimes even the most ethical person can make the most unethical choice."

"Is that what you think I did?" I asked him.

He smiled a sad smile. "Perhaps that would be overstating the case. I suppose what I feel is . . . that I failed you somehow."

I looked at his large hands resting on his pant legs. Those hands that had held me when I was sad and comforted me when I was sick. "You didn't fail me," I whispered. "How can I make you understand? Something wonderful has happened," I said, looking earnestly at my parents. "Monroe is . . . he's terrific. You completely misjudge him. I don't want you to be hurt by that," I added quickly.

"Oh, Sandra," my mother said with exasperation.

"I know he ran out on you, Mom," I continued quickly, "but he explained why—"

"Did he?" my mother asked dryly.

"He did," I insisted. "He's clean and sober now, everything has changed. And he is the most wonderful musician. He wrote a song for me, and he has a new CD out in Europe."

"He always could charm the leaves off the trees," my mother murmured. "But I thought you'd be too smart to fall for his line."

"It's not a line!" I insisted. "He's changed! Can't you believe that a person can change?"

"Baby, that man left me with no money and a child to raise by myself," my mother said. "I think it's awfully convenient that he's coming around to see you after all the hard work is done."

I stood up. "Well, I'm sorry if that's how you see it," I said stiffly. "The way I see it is that you and Monroe are two terrific people who were never meant to be together. You wanted a laid-back life and security; he wanted to follow his dream, no matter what."

"I guess it's a good thing one of us wanted security," my mother said bitterly, "or you wouldn't have had a home."

"Yes, I would," I insisted. "It just would have been a different kind of home." I picked up my purse and looped the strap over my shoulder. "I love you both, but I'm not going to choose between you two and Monroe. Because now I love him, too."

I got up and had started up the stairs when Larry called to me.

"Sandra?"

I turned around.

"You don't have to choose, child," he said softly. "Please don't ever think that we're asking you to choose."

My mother reached for Larry's hand, but he didn't look at her. His eyes, filled with love and hurt and disappointment, followed me up the stairs.

I took a long, hot shower, letting the water cascade over me. Then I wrapped myself up in my favorite oversized pink flannel robe and got into bed. I stared up at the ceiling, my hands under my head, and I willed myself to concentrate on the thrill of victory and forget about the conversation I'd just had with my parents. Wild Hearts was going to be in the state finals for the Battle of the Bands. I was determined to ignore my guilt feelings, and I concentrated hard on not thinking about my parents at all. I wasn't going to let my victory be sullied by their anger and disappointment in me.

It was really, really hard, though. I knew I had hurt them, and perfect people do not hurt their parents. Perfection was a habit, you see, deeply ingrained.

I closed my eyes and saw my mother's face, angry and betrayed, and Larry's face, so hurt and confused.

Why did it all have to be so difficult?

Well, maybe Sandra Farrell wasn't quite so perfect, and maybe that was perfectly okay.

On impulse I sat up and dialed the number of Monroe's hotel, which I knew by heart. Being a musician, he was a night person, so I figured he'd be up. I wanted to tell him one more time how much his support meant to me, and make a date to see him the next day. Maybe I'd take him over to meet Darryl. It was about time they got to know each other. No matter how much Darryl and I fought, I knew he loved me more than anything or anyone in the world.

I had the operator ring Monroe's room. But after ten rings, I finally just left a message for him at the desk. Maybe he was in the shower or down in the bar having something nonalcoholic, I figured.

I closed my eyes and relived that wonderful moment when the emcee had called our names, and then the even more unbelievable moment when we realized we had actually come in second. Six hundred dollars! Wild Hearts was actually going to have money in the bank!

I jumped off my bed and got my purse. I was going to spread all the money out on my bed and just stare at it. But when I rummaged around in my purse, I couldn't find the envelope. I looked again. Nothing. But that was crazy. My heart started to beat a rapid, anxious tattoo in my chest. I dumped my purse out on my bed and pushed the contents around until I could see everything.

There was no envelope. There was no six hundred dollars.

But that just couldn't be.

I went over the chain of events in my head. First Savy had handed me the envelope with the four hundred dollars in it when we were onstage. Then when we got switched to second place I could see myself taking that envelope of money. I remembered putting it into my purse in the dressing room before I went out onstage for that last photo.

Had it fallen out at the Green Hills Grille?

But no. I had been about to unzip my purse to get money to pay for my food when Savy told me that her parents were paying for everyone. So I had never gone into my purse at all.

Could someone have stolen that money? But no one had been around when I put it into my purse, and after we left the dressing room my purse had never been out of my sight.

And then it hit me.

Someone had been around.

Monroe.

Monroe was the only one in the dressing room with me when I put that money into my purse. Then I left the dressing room.

And I left him alone with the money.

I flashed on his face, as his eyes had flicked to my pocket where the money was stashed. What had he said? That he wasn't a perfect person? What had he meant by that? And what had he been so upset about?

Even as I threw off my robe and scrambled into a pair of jeans and a sweatshirt, I didn't believe Monroe really had taken Wild Hearts' money. I couldn't believe it. I wouldn't believe it.

I stuffed everything back into my purse and ran downstairs. Fortunately my mom and

Larry had gone to bed, so I didn't have to do any explaining. I grabbed a jacket and ran out to my Jeep.

I pounded on the door to Monroe's room as hard as I could. I kicked the door. No answer.

But it couldn't be. It just couldn't be.

I ran back down to the lobby.

"Do you know when Mr. LaCrue is scheduled to check out?" I asked the desk clerk breathlessly.

She checked her computer. "Mr. LaCrue has already checked out," she informed me.

"But . . . that can't be," I said, stunned.

"That's what the computer shows," she said.

"Maybe . . . maybe he just did the paperwork ahead of time," I tried desperately. "Maybe you saw him tonight—a handsome black man, late thirties . . ." I tried to recall what Monroe had worn to the show. "He was wearing black Levi's and a black and red silk shirt?"

"Oh, yes, I do remember him," the clerk said cheerfully. "I remember complimenting him on his shirt. He definitely checked out. He left about an hour ago."

No physical pain could have hurt me as

deeply as the pain of hearing those words. I gulped hard. I was not going to cry in the lobby of the hotel in front of this chirpy, perfectly groomed clerk.

"Did he leave a forwarding address?" I asked quietly.

She checked the computer again. "No, he didn't. I'm sorry."

I was numb. As the tears threatened my eyes, I turned and headed for the door. One foot in front of the other. That was all I could do.

"Oh, miss!" the clerk called to me.

I turned around.

"Are you Mr. LaCrue's daughter, by any chance?"

Hearing that sent the knife deeper into my heart. I nodded mutely, my vision blurred by tears.

"He left a note for you," she said, holding out an envelope.

I took it from the clerk and hurried out to my Jeep, where I could read the note without anyone seeing me fall apart. Then by the lights in the parking lot, I read his letter.

Dearest daughter,
By now you know I'm gone, and you

know I've taken your money. No matter how much you think you hate me, I hate myself more. What I'm about to tell you doesn't excuse me, but I hope it will help you to understand.

Before I left France, my lady friend found a lump in her breast. The biopsy was done while I was here with you. The day before yesterday I got a call from her telling me she has cancer. Tomorrow she goes into surgery. The doctors say the cancer has already spread to her lymph nodes and her liver, and her chances don't look very good.

I'm not a strong man, Sandra. When I heard that news, I went out and got a drink. No, I went out and got drunk. I'm not proud of that, but there it is. Once I got drunk, the cocaine just seemed to follow. And cocaine is an expensive drug. You see, Sandra, I just don't know how to carry on without her.

I am on my way back to France to be with Marie. I will always love you. And I promise, I will send this money back to you.

I suppose I never really deserved to have you love me. Maybe I just needed to ruin everything and prove that to myself once and for all. I am sorry I'm not the father you deserve. You will always be the child of my heart.

Love,
Your father, Monroe LaCrue

It was the worst moment of my life. I sobbed as if my heart was breaking, because it was.

What was I going to do? How could I tell my parents and Darryl that they'd been right all along, that Monroe was a liar and a thief and a drug addict, that he'd stolen money from the band?

Oh, God, the band! The six hundred dollars! What was I going to do about the six hundred dollars? Panic clutched at my stomach. How could I ever repay the band that money? I had about eighty dollars to my name, and a bunch of bonds that I couldn't touch until college.

I felt so sick that I quickly opened the car door and retched, sobs racking my body. I cried and retched until I felt empty, empty of everything except a dull pain that I knew I would feel forever.

I had to think of a plan. I would get a part-time job, and I'd work however long it took to pay back the band.

Meanwhile, if I got a serious part-time job on top of everything else I was doing, I would be so busy I'd have to quit the band. Or quit school.

What I really felt like doing was quitting my entire life.

I couldn't tell anyone the truth about what had happened. But I couldn't lie, either.

And then a thought dawned on me.

There was only one person who could save my butt. One person who could help me through this crisis, loan me the money without missing it, and keep my secret while I slowly earned the money back by working at the gym.

Kimmy.

Kimmy was rich. Very rich. But she was the person in the band I was the least close to. Besides, she had absolutely no reason to help me out.

Still, what choice did I have?

I had to swallow my pride and go to Kimmy.

I turned my watch until it caught the lights in the parking lot. It was two o'clock in the morning.

I went back in the hotel, raced over to a pay phone, and dialed Kimmy's private number. The phone rang and rang.

"Hello?" her sleep-filled voice finally answered.

"Kimmy, it's Sandra," I said with no preamble. "I'm in trouble. I need some help."

"What is it?" she asked, sounding instantly alert. "Should I call the police?"

"No," I replied, clutching the phone hard. "But I need to talk to you. Can I come over there?"

"Yes, yes, of course," she agreed. "I'll call the guard at the gate so he knows to let you in."

"Thanks, Kimmy," I said as the tears began to leak out of my eyes again.

"I'll be waiting for you," she promised.

CHAPTER
12

*P*ragmatism is good. You face reality and then you deal with it. That's always been my motto.

I told Kimmy everything, and she agreed to help me. She would take the six hundred dollars out of her bank account and give it to me, and she would keep my secret. I vowed to pay her back, and she accepted my promise gracefully, saying there was no hurry and I shouldn't kill myself trying to do it.

She also told me I was making a big mistake by not confiding in the rest of the band. I disagreed, and we left it at that.

After that, I vowed to just go on with my life. To just cut Monroe out of it. Good-bye, good riddance, *sayonara*. He would be nothing more than a bad memory, until finally I wouldn't even remember him at all.

I was extra nice to my parents, and after a couple of days they warmed up to me. I told them Monroe had gone back to Europe. Then I added a stupid lie. I told them he was coming to see me again in the spring.

I don't know why I did that.

Darryl called and we made a date for a couple of days later. Even though it was midweek, there were teachers' conferences, so we wouldn't have school the next day. I apologized for walking out on him at the restaurant, and he apologized for walking out on me at the Battle of the Bands. I asked him why he did it, and he said he was just trying to be nice to my parents because they were so upset. I decided to let it slide.

So you see, I really had everything under control. Oh, I admit I read Monroe's letter over and over, and I kept it under my pillow with his photo.

But that didn't mean it was affecting me.

Darryl and I went roller-skating at a giant rink in Brentwood. It was the perfect choice of something to do—nothing heavy, just crazy fun. I'm an excellent skater, but Darryl is terrible. As rock oldies blared through the sound system, he kept grabbing on to me as he faltered on his skates. Sometimes I righted him, sometimes we both went crashing to the floor, laughing hysterically.

Someone started a limbo skating contest, and Darryl and I entered. Darryl was out on his second pass under the bamboo stick. I hung in there until a little girl with red pigtails went so low that her back was practically hitting the floor. I came in second—and won a blue stuffed bunny.

We pigged out on hot dogs afterward, then we went for a drive near the river. I felt happy and content. Darryl pulled his old car up close to the water and turned off the ignition. Then he turned to me and took me in his arms.

"I really missed you," he told me, and gave me a delicious kiss.

"I missed you, too," I replied, once my lips were free to speak.

"Are your parents getting over being mad?" he asked me.

I nodded. "You were right. I should have just told them the truth in the first place."

He kissed the tip of my nose. "See, that's one of the many reasons I love you. You aren't afraid to admit when you're wrong."

"Well, I'm not wrong all that often," was my retort.

He laughed and kissed me again.

"Hey, you didn't mention what you thought of Wild Hearts," I asked him lightly.

"Ya'll are good," he replied. "I mean, that kind of music doesn't really speak to me—I guess you know that—but I could tell how good you are."

"Big of you to admit it," I teased.

He reached for my ribs and tickled me. "You have tons of talent, even if you are a pain."

I shrieked and dodged his hand. "Stop! No tickling!"

He pulled me to him and kissed me again. "Okay," he murmured huskily. "Is this better?"

"Much," I said, and gave myself up to kissing him.

"I'm sorry I didn't get to know Monroe before he left," Darryl said when he pulled away from me.

"Really?" I asked with surprise. I had casually told Darryl that Monroe had gone back to Europe, as if everything between my father and me was fine.

"Maybe I was a little harsh," Darryl admitted. "I mean, you love him. So I'd like to know him."

I smiled at him, loving his handsome, serious face. I refused to even think about Monroe and how he'd betrayed me. I would think about Darryl instead. "Just when I start to think you're a moron, you turn around and say something wonderful."

"We aim to please," Darryl said, nuzzling my neck.

And then the strangest words popped out of my mouth. "When Monroe comes back in the spring, the three of us can go out together," I heard myself say. It was the same lie I'd told my parents.

"That's when he'll be back, huh?" Darryl asked.

I nodded. "We'll go out to dinner. You'll really like him. He's nothing like what my mother thinks."

"In other words there are two sides to every story," Darryl translated.

I peered at him in the darkness. "You were so . . . so dogmatic before, so sure you knew better. What changed your mind?"

He shrugged. "Hearing your band play, maybe. It was like all of a sudden all the things I was thinking about what you should do or shouldn't do didn't make sense anymore. I mean, there you were up there, and you were really, really good. And I thought to myself, If God has given my baby that kind of talent, who am I to say she shouldn't use it?"

"Oh, Darryl . . ." I sighed lovingly.

"And then that started me thinking about everything else," Darryl continued earnestly. "You were right, Sandra. I don't have any right to tell you what to do."

"Even though you love to," I teased him.

"Yeah," he agreed with a laugh. "Even though I love to."

I snuggled close to him. "Did I mention how much I love you?"

"No, you did not," he replied archly. "How much?"

"To infinity," I stated magnificently, throwing my arms wide.

"Hmmm, that's not enough," Darryl decided.

"Oh, it isn't? So what would be enough?"

He contemplated that a second. "How about enough to strip off all your clothes this instant and go skinny-dipping with me in that river?"

"We can't do that!" I shrieked with a laugh. "It's not even legal to swim here!"

"Okay, then, let's compromise," Darryl said. "Just strip off all your clothes."

"Ha-ha," I said, but I burst into bubbles of laughter. This was the Darryl I had fallen in love with. I leaned over and kissed him, sure he would know exactly how I felt.

The way he kissed me back told me he did.

"Just make yourself comfortable," I called to Darryl as I undressed in my bathroom.

We had driven back to my house, and I was shivering all the way. The night had turned cold, and somehow I'd gotten very chilled. I wanted nothing more than to jump into a hot shower. Darryl often hung out in my room— my parents trusted us completely—so he agreed to wait while I showered. Then we were planning to watch a late movie together on TV.

I sang "It Wasn't God Who Made Honky Tonk Angels" to myself as I showered, feeling better than I'd felt in a long time. Darryl and I were okay again, my parents were pretty much back to normal, my grades were basically back on tract, and even Jennie Neuman seemed to be lying low. And then there was Wild Hearts. We were in the state finals for the Battle of the Bands. Anything was possible!

So what if Monroe had turned out to be a loser after all? That was his problem, not mine.

I toweled myself dry and splashed on my

favorite after-bath cologne, then I pulled on some sweats and padded back into my room, towel-drying my hair. "How about if we pop some corn?" I suggested. "We could melt some butter and—"

Then I caught the look on Darryl's face.

And saw what was in his hands.

Monroe's letter to me.

"Where did you get that?" I asked, grabbing it away from him. "That's private."

"I already read it, Sandra."

"Well, you had no right to," I told him, my face burning. I stuck the letter in the top drawer of my dresser and kept my back to Darryl so he wouldn't see how badly I was shaking.

"It was lying out on your bed," he explained. "It was in plain sight."

"It was private," I whispered, still holding on to the dresser for dear life.

I felt Darryl come up behind me. He put his hands on my shoulders. "I'm so sorry, Sandra," he said quietly. "I'm sorry he hurt you."

"He didn't hurt me," I replied, but the tears that began falling from my eyes belied my words.

Darryl turned me around and held me in his arms, as my body was racked by sobs.

"I could kill him," Darryl said, his voice harsh with emotion. "I could just kill him."

I finally got hold of myself, and we sat down together on my bed. I blew my nose hard and took a few deep breaths.

"What are you doing about the money?" Darryl asked me.

I told him about Kimmy.

"Huh, well, that's impressive," Darryl admitted. "Of course, she's rich, she won't even know it's gone," he added.

"I'm going to pay her back," I explained, still wiping at my eyes.

"When do you think you're going to find the time to make that kind of money?" Darryl asked me archly.

"I'll do it slowly," I said. "But I'll do it. It's my responsibility."

"No, it isn't," Darryl said. "It's that skunk who passed himself off as your father."

"He's not a skunk," I said.

"I can't believe you're defending him!" Darryl exclaimed. "As far as I'm concerned he is low beyond low!"

"It's not his fault," I insisted.

"Sandra, wake up and smell the coffee, baby!" Darryl exclaimed. "This guy is a user and a leech, a useless human being! A thief

178

and a parasite! Why did you tell me he was coming back here in the spring?"

"I don't know," I replied miserably.

"It's not like you to fantasize, baby," Darryl admonished me.

"I'm telling you I don't know why I said it, okay?" I cried. "Just leave it alone!"

"Did you tell your mom and Larry what happened?"

"No," I admitted.

"Sandra! What are you thinking?" Darryl exploded.

"Look, it's my decision," I said. "I don't want to tell them."

Darryl jumped up and paced around the room. "I just don't believe this! You were telling me earlier that you were wrong not to tell them the truth before, and here you go and lie to them again!"

"It's none of their business!" I yelled, jumping up to face him. "Or yours either, for that matter!"

"Would you just listen to yourself?" Darryl asked, taking me by the shoulders.

"How about if you listen to yourself?" I shot back, stepping out of his grasp. "How about how you weren't going to tell me what to do anymore!"

He dropped his hands, and the heat seemed to go out of him. "You're right," he agreed, and sat down on my bed. He seemed to be fighting to control himself. "I'm sorry. It's just that I love you so much."

He looked up at me and I went over to sit by him. I took his hand in mine.

"Your parents really, really love you, Sandra."

"I know that."

"They'll understand," he said gently.

"I just can't tell them yet, Darryl. Eventually, maybe. But ... not yet."

He sighed. "Okay," he finally said. "Do what you have to do."

I kissed him. "I'm sorry I yelled."

"Me too."

"I'm completely exhausted," I told him, and leaned my head against his chest.

"Maybe I should leave and let you just go on to sleep," Darryl suggested. "Come on, I'll tuck you in."

Without protest I got under the covers, and Darryl tucked me in and kissed me on the forehead as if I were his precious little girl.

Like the kind of love I'd never gotten from Monroe. And now I never would.

I felt so sad at that moment. My daddy. He

had told me he would always be in my life, and he had lied.

And there was nothing I could do about it, except hurt.

Darryl kissed me again, wiped the tears from my cheeks, and crooned something silly to me as if I were about four years old.

For just this once, I didn't mind.

The next morning I studied like a demon, then I went over to Savy's for a band meeting.

The first thing Kimmy did was to take me aside and give me a certified check for six hundred dollars. What could I say? I just slipped it into my purse and planned to go to the bank right after our meeting to open our bank account.

"I still think you should tell them," Kimmy said quietly.

"I can't," I replied. "I just can't."

Kimmy nodded. "I understand. But if you change your mind ... well, I just want you to know that I'll be right there for you," she added shyly.

I felt a lump in my throat. Maybe I had underestimated Kimmy. "Thanks," I said, and we headed back into the music room.

Everyone was very excited about planning

for the statewide Battle of the Bands. Although it was quite a ways off, we talked about what songs we should do, what we should wear, and what we should spend our six hundred dollars on.

"Publicity shots," Savy said firmly.

"Forget that," Jane argued. "We need really good demo tapes!"

"How about if we just leave the money in the bank for a little while and chill on this?" I suggested. "The money isn't going anywhere."

"Well, I know this guy who told me he'd do our photos for free," Savy said. "And all we have to do is pay for the prints. If we don't like the shots, we don't pay anything. It's a totally no-lose deal!"

"Is he a decent photographer?" Jane asked skeptically.

"I don't actually know," Savy admitted. "But he's a great bass player!" she added with a twinkle in her eye.

"Who?" Kimmy asked.

"Oh, you might remember him," Savy said nonchalantly. "Ryan Black? The bass player from Jack Flash?"

Kimmy's eyes got wide. "Did he call you?"

"Sort of," Savy replied. "I mean, he's called me, and he's stopped over a few times, actually."

"Why didn't you tell me?" Kimmy asked Savy.

"Well, there hasn't been anything to tell," Savy said. "Yet," she added mischievously.

"Oh, this is great," Jane groaned. "You're going to become a couple. I just know it. Then all three of you will have boyfriends, and I will still be guy-free. A date-less, kiss-less slug crawling slowly across the face of humanity."

"That's certainly how I think of you," I deadpanned.

"Ryan isn't my boyfriend," Savy insisted. "Although I can't say there aren't possibilities. Anyway, can he take shots of us?"

"Sure." Jane sighed grudgingly. "I bet he'll make *you* look terrific."

We kidded around about guys for a while—I told them Darryl and I had kissed and made up. Kimmy told us about her last date with Sawyer—very hot—and Savy told us a hilarious story about the worst guy she ever kissed.

Then Jane jumped up and ran over to her purse. "Oh, I almost forgot! I have a major surprise!" She pulled something from her purse and brandished it in the air. "Ta-da!" She waved around a cassette tape.

"What's that?" Savy asked.

"I was talking to my best friend back in New

York from when I still had a life, Anita Lebo-witz," Jane said. "And I asked her if she re-membered that jazz class we took—Anita is a jazz freak," Jane explained. "Anyway, it turned out that Anita made her own tapes of all the stuff we heard in that class—including Monroe's demo of 'Lost Child'! I just about freaked when she told me! So I asked her to make me a copy, and here it is!"

"Put it on!" Savy exclaimed.

Jane ran over to the tape deck while Kimmy and I traded looks. I took deep breaths and forced myself to maintain control.

But as soon as I heard the voice of my father singing those lyrics, the lyrics he'd written for me, I lost it. Tears coursed down my cheeks. A sob tore from my gut.

Jane stopped the tape.

Everyone stared at me.

And then the truth came pouring out of my mouth.

"I can't believe he did it," I sobbed. "I still can't believe it!" Kimmy brought me over a box of Kleenex, and I plucked out a handful.

"Neither can I," Jane said in a stunned voice. "Wow."

"So the six hundred dollars is gone?" Savy asked in a small voice.

I shook my head. "I told Kimmy the truth about what happened. She's lending us the money. But I swear I'll pay her back every penny!"

"Wow," Jane said again. "You just never know, huh?"

"The part about Monroe's girlfriend being sick, is that true?" Savy asked.

"Yeah—that is, if his letter is the truth," I managed. "I mean, who knows?" I pulled Monroe's letter out of my purse—I stored it there now for safekeeping—and I handed it to Savy. She sat down next to me on the couch and read it out loud to everyone. Then she handed it back to me wordlessly.

Jane came and sat on the other side of me. "It sucks," she said quietly.

Kimmy plopped herself down near my feet. "Yeah, it does," she agreed.

"Darryl found that letter," I sniffed, tucking it back into my purse. "He got really mad at me because I haven't told my parents the truth about Monroe."

"Well, the way I look at it is, this isn't the same as lying to them about whether or not you're seeing him," Jane mused. "I mean, you're not exactly lying to them. You just haven't told them why he left town."

"Right," Savy agreed. "And you don't have to, either."

"I let them think he was wonderful," I said in a low voice. "I let them think they were wrong about him and I was right."

Kimmy patted my shoe. "Don't be so hard on yourself, Sandra," she said. "I think you should take all the time you need. It's like . . . it's like you have to give yourself time to grieve or something, you know? Like you have to let go of who you thought Monroe was."

Jane looked down at Kimmy and raised her eyebrows. "Since when did you get so smart?"

"Oh, I've always been real smart for other people," Kimmy drawled in her soft voice. "It's only for myself that I get all messed up."

"Listen," Savy said. "I don't think you should have to be responsible because Monroe stole our money. I mean, it wasn't your fault."

"But—" I began to protest.

"As far as I'm concerned, we can just give Kimmy back her money and start over," Savy continued.

"I told you you should have given that money to me," Jane reminded us.

I managed a small smile. "You guys are being wonderful, but I *do* feel responsible and I *will* do something about it."

"In what lifetime?" Jane asked. "You're totally overextended as it is!"

"I'd like to make an offer," Kimmy said. "How about if the band keeps the six hundred dollars so we have some working capital? We'll all pretend that we didn't win any money—I'll just be making an investment in the band. And Sandra won't have to pay me back."

"No, absolutely not—" I said.

"Wait, hold up," Kimmy said. "Now, if we place in the statewide Battle of the Bands, we win megabucks, right? So then the band would pay me back my investment, and we'd still have some money in the bank. How's that?"

"And if we don't place, I'll find a way to pay you back every penny?" I asked Kimmy.

"Deal," Kimmy said. "What do ya'll think?"

"Makes sense to me," Jane agreed.

"Me, too," Savy said, grinning at her best friend. "You are a very cool girl, Kimmy Carrier."

I smiled at all of them. "And I am very, very lucky to have you as my friends," I said humbly.

"That's true," Jane agreed. "Now, how about if we work on trying to find me the perfect guy? I would love to make my ex-boyfriend, Chad, drool with envy. "How about if we—"

Just then the phone rang. Savy picked up the extension on the end table.

"Hello? . . . Uh-huh. . . . Uh-huh. Just a sec, I'll get her." She put her hand over the mouthpiece of the phone. "It's Jennie Neuman from school," Savy told me. "She said she called your house and your mom gave her this number."

"It must be junior class stuff," I said, taking the phone from Savy. "Hello?"

"Sandra, I'm so sorry to bother you at your little band rehearsal," Jennie drawled. "But I just felt I couldn't wait to speak with you."

"What's up?" I asked briskly.

"Are you sitting down?" she asked me.

"Yes, Jennie, I'm sitting down," I said. "What is it?"

"Well, you know I just hate to be the bearer of bad tidings, but I felt I had to tell you this as a friend and a fellow junior class officer. You remember I told you about that petition to have you impeached as president of the junior class?"

"Yes," I said, my heartbeat speeding up in my chest.

"It's got a whole lot of signatures on it now," Jennie said. "I felt you should know."

"And I bet your name is right at the top of

the list, right, Jennie?" I asked her in a bitter voice.

"Well, I don't think we need to get into personalities here," Jennie replied. "But you might want to consider stepping down—for the good of the class, you know."

"Jennie," I said, clutching the phone hard, "I am not a quitter. The only thing I intend to step down on is your lying, smug, self-satisfied face. Have I made myself clear?"

"Well!" Jennie humphed indignantly. "I have never been so—"

But I didn't hear the rest because I had the satisfaction of slamming the phone down in her ear.

"What the hell was that?" Savy asked.

I told them. "I should have known when Jennie was all sweet and docile the last few days that she was just setting me up for the kill," I said.

"The whole thing is ridiculous!" Savy exclaimed. "No one is going to impeach you! She just got a few of her friends to sign some stupid thing. Forget about it!"

"You think?" I asked doubtfully.

"I know," Savy said with certainty. "She and Katie Lynn like to think they run the school, but they're a big joke!"

"I have a theory," Jane began, "that God doles out these pastel people types across America. Every high school has some of them. Then they marry each other and breed, and a whole new pastel generation fans out to uglify the life of every teen who has ever had an original thought."

"Uglify?" Savy repeated, laughing hysterically. "That is so southern!"

"No, no!" Jane shrieked, pretending to stab herself in the heart. "Accuse me of anything, but don't accuse me of being southern!"

Everyone started laughing and carrying on, teasing each other about one thing or another. And it was funny, but I felt happy and sad, both at the same time. Compared to the pain I felt about Monroe, Jennie and her stupid petition paled. That petition did worry me, though. Still, I knew that whatever happened, I had these three amazing friends to stand by me.

I didn't need to pretend with them. I didn't need to be perfect for them. And they loved me just the same.

It was almost enough to make me let them call me Sandy.

Almost. But not quite.

EPILOGUE

For the next few days I really concentrated on my schoolwork and my tennis. The band had agreed to take a week off so everyone could catch up on other things. I got an A on my next English paper and an A-minus on a calculus quiz.

For three days in a row I hit tennis balls until I could barely lift my arm. Then I did the challenge match with Janine that the coach had insisted we play.

I crushed her, six-four, six-two, thank-you-very-much.

Of course there was still the little matter of Jennie Neuman and her gang of fools to contend with. I called a class officers' meeting for the following Monday, figuring I'd tackle the problem head on. If there really was some long list of names of people who wanted me out, I would just have to face it. And if there wasn't, then Jennie Neuman was going to have to get out of my face.

Things were good with my parents and pretty great with Darryl. He even sent me roses for no good reason.

So you can see I was back on top, handling everything.

Until the day I came home from school and was going over some history notes in the living room when the doorbell rang. I padded to the door and opened it.

"Federal Express," the deliveryman said. "Sign for it right here."

I signed, thanked him, and took the package into the living room.

And then I had to sit down. Because the return address said Paris, France.

It was from my father.

With trembling fingers I pulled open the large envelope, and shook the contents out.

Six one-hundred-dollar bills fluttered to the rug.

Followed by a red heart on a key chain, engraved with the name Miles Davis.

It was stupid of me, I guess, to think I was all over the pain, that I could just handle everything. I cried so hard that day, bitter tears, lonely tears, abandoned tears.

But as I held that heart in my hand and looked down at my father's address in Paris, I knew it wasn't over. He loved me. I knew he did. And for better or worse I loved him now too.

It wasn't easy, facing up to how flawed he was. And it wasn't easy to admit that I could still love him, even as badly as he'd hurt me.

And in a funny way, it made me appreciate my mom and Larry. They were the ones who stood by me and were always there for me. I needed to tell them how much I appreciated them and loved them. They were my real parents. And Larry was my real father. But so was Monroe. I guess now I would have two. And that would be okay.

Right then I made a few decisions. I was going to tell my mom and Larry the truth about Monroe. I was going to be honest with them about whatever decisions I made concerning him in the future. And I was going to write to Monroe in France.

With Monroe's heart clasped firmly in my hand, I went upstairs to compose two letters.

The first was to my parents, to tell them how much I loved them. The second was to my birth father.

I wouldn't give up on him.

After all, it didn't matter which one of us grew up first, really, did it?

I would take the first step.

Heart to Heart
~ ♥ ♥ ~

Dear Cherie,

I have said it before and I'll say it again, CHERIE BENNETT IS A FABULOUS AUTHOR! WILD HEARTS books are so good they leave me in a daze. I loved WILD HEARTS FOREVER, and I couldn't believe how it turned out. I think this book had a lot to do with betrayal. I'm glad you wrote a book dealing with drugs. You write about real teen problems and how to solve them. In your books not everything is perfect, just like the real world! WILD HEARTS FOREVER!

> *One of your biggest fans,*
> *Sarah Lindsay Sasser*
> *Nashville, Tennessee*

Dear Sarah,

I agree with you, WILD HEARTS FOREVER was about betrayal. Sometimes a guy who seems to be wonderful and perfect turns out to be anything but! And sometimes we fall in love with what we want someone to be, and not who they really are! Yes, I've been down love's bumpy highway myself—and lived to tell the tale! Have any of you ever fallen for a guy who betrayed you? Write and tell us about it!

> Best,
> Cherie

Dear Cherie,

I love your new series WILD HEARTS and I also love the SUNSET ISLAND series. I really think you should continue both of them! Savy Leeman is my favorite character. My friends and I think you write the best books. How do you get your ideas? Wild Hearts forever!

Sincerely,
Tracy Chan
Walnut, CA

Dear Tracy,

I promise to keep writing both series as long as all of you out there keep reading! The question I get asked most often is: "Where do you get your ideas?" I get ideas from my own personal experiences, experiences of friends, TV, the newspaper, and most especially from the letters I receive from all of you out there! Hey, you guys are the source! You write and share with me your thoughts, worries, hopes, and dreams, and I try to address those issues in my books.

Best,
Cherie

Dear Cherie,

I absolutely love WILD HEARTS! I can really relate with Kimmy. All my friends always tell me I have a good voice, but I have a hard time believing them. Then we were having solo tryouts for the advanced singing group at my school, and I couldn't believe it when I got it! Now I realize that I do have talent, just like Kimmy. I am going to read all the new WILD HEARTS books you write, and I usually finish one in about two days, so please write fast!

Devoted Reader,
Jenn Wish
Agoura Hills, CA

Dear Jenn,

Congrats on getting the solo! I am so happy for you! Listen, I know how hard it is to put yourself out there and risk failure—believe me when I tell you that I've failed at many things, many times, and it hurts. But I absolutely believe that the only true failure is not to try at all. So when those negative voices start to fill your head—you know what I mean, that little devil that sits on your shoulder and tells you you can't succeed, and who do you think you are to try, and all that—DON'T LISTEN! Follow your dreams, reach for the stars. It's worth it!

Best,
Cherie

Dear Readers,

Time to catch up, so let me tell you what's been going on in my life lately. A play of mine just opened here in Nashville, and I'm happy to say it got really good reviews. Let me tell you, it is so nerve-wracking to wait for those reviews to come out!! It's like one person has all this power to judge me in print, and even if I tell myself it's only one person's opinion, it's really hard not to care. Okay, it's impossible, so I'm reeeaaaal happy that I got good reviews! Have any of you aspiring writers out there tried writing plays? I know of a really great teen play contest in New York City you can enter, so if you're interested, write to me, and I'll write back and tell you all the details. It was great fun to see some WILD HEARTS fans at my play, including Sarah Sasser, Jennie Smith, and Lana Taradash. All three of these incredibly cool girls are talented young actresses with major futures ahead of them. You know what I say—always follow your dreams!

My mom recently had serious emergency surgery, which was very scary. It came as a complete surprise. She's always been totally healthy. She's having more surgery next week. And you know, it's weird. I mean, I always just took her good health for granted. I can't imagine anything really awful happening to her. It's so frightening when a parent gets seriously ill. I'm sure some of you have had to deal with this—which is even harder if you're a teen. I'd love to hear from you about the experience—maybe I can write about it in a future WILD HEARTS.

So . . . what about the next WILD HEARTS book, huh? Well, it's called WILD HEARTS: PASSIONATE KISSES (I have to tell you, I love the title!) and Jane is about to fall hard and fast for a guy who comes from a totally different world than her own. Can love conquer all? What do you all think out there?

I can't tell you how much I appreciate all your enthusiasm for the girls of WILD HEARTS. You tell me that Jane, Kimmy, Savy, and Sandra seem like real people to you. Well, they're real to me, too! I love hearing from all of you. Your letters mean so much to me. As always, I promise to personally answer each and every letter. Just let me know if I can consider yours for publication. If it's private, that's fine, too—just let me know.

Thank you again for being so terrific.

Wild Hearts forever!

Cherie Bennett

Cherie Bennett
c/o Archway Paperbacks
Pocket Books
1230 Avenue of the Americas
New York, NY 10020